THE AUTHOR

Alexander Sutherland Neill was born in 1883 in Forfar, Strathmore, Scotland, and educated at his father's village school. At fourteen he became an office boy, then a draper's assistant, before training as a teacher and reading English at Edinburgh University. By the start of the First World War he was headmaster of Gretna Green School where his disillusionment with conventional education, expressed so delightfully in *A Dominie's Log* (1915), led to his dismissal. He continued to write – *A Dominie Dismissed* (1916), *The Booming of Bunkie* and *A Dominie in Doubt* (both 1920), – and taught in Hampstead, London, until 1921, when he helped start the International School at Hellorau, near Dresden. In 1924 he set up his own school in Austria, then brought it to England, establishing the famous Summerhill in Lyme Regis, Dorset, and later in Leiston, Suffolk, a school run according to his passionate beliefs in the need for teaching reform.

Neill's constant battle with accepted notions, and his astonishing success with difficult children, made the educational world take notice. He carried forward the debate on 'progressive education' in lively books such as *The Problem Child* (1926), *The Problem Parent* (1932), *The Problem Teacher* (1939), *Hearts Not Heads* (1945), *The Free Child* (1953), *Summerhill* (1962) and his autobiography *Neill! Neill! Orange Peel* (1973). Married twice, he had one daughter. Having 'no money to retire', he worked on at Summerhill until his death, at Aldeburgh, in 1973. As *The Times* said in his obituary, 'If children are happier nowadays in school than their elders sometimes were it is due in no small measure to this craggy, lovable Scot.'

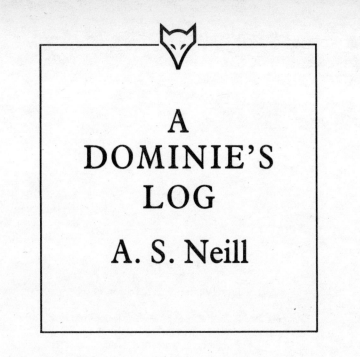

A
DOMINIE'S
LOG

A. S. Neill

New Introduction by
Hugh MacKenzie

THE HOGARTH PRESS
LONDON

Published in 1986 by
The Hogarth Press
Chatto & Windus Ltd
40 William IV Street, London WC2N 4DF

First published in Great Britain by Herbert Jenkins Ltd 1915
Hogarth edition offset from the original British edition
Copyright the Estate of A. S. Neill
Introduction copyright © Hugh MacKenzie 1986

British Library Cataloguing in Publication Data

Neill, A. S.
A dominie's log
1. Neill, A.S.
2. Summerhill School – Biography
3. Teachers – Great Britain – Biography
I. Title
371.2'012'0924   LS795.L6

ISBN 0 7012 0644 6

Printed in Great Britain by
Cox & Wyman Ltd
Reading, Berkshire

INTRODUCTION

To meet one's hero in the flesh can prove rather an unnerving and disappointing experience. I faced up to the prospect back in the late Fifties when I was fortunate enough to persuade A. S. Neill, a major, if not *the* major, figure of the education movement this century, to return to his native country to lecture about Summerhill – the school he founded in Dorset (it later moved to Suffolk) in 1925, and a place which must have been a delight for any child. I looked forward to an evening in the company of a man of inspired ideas and rare humour – the raconteur I had come to expect from the pages of *A Dominie's Log*; but not without trepidation.

In those days, I was a geography teacher and had, early in my career, been influenced by Neill's pioneering philosophy; a philosophy founded on the twin pillars of self-discipline for the child and the total abolition of corporal punishment. (It is interesting to reflect, however, that I was introduced to his works not at Moray House, the Edinburgh teacher training college, but in the officers' mess at RAF White Waltham, where I went on to do my National Service.) His books completely altered my view of education – as it has those of so many others, teachers, pupils and parents alike. His emphasis on the importance of play in childhood, the self-pacing of learning (or individualised learning, as it is now called), on democratic assemblies where teacher and pupil meet as equals and, most important, his belief that education should be enjoyable – a heresy to some, not least in his Calvinist Scotland – have sustained me throughout my career. Most of these tenets are now to be found in some degree in state schools, although in this country they may be threatened by the current drift back to basics and Victorian values. And in my work these days as Headteacher of Craigroyston Community High

School in Edinburgh and as a director of a Bernard van Leer project for Community Education, I have always tried to embrace them.

But all this was a long way off when I first met Neill in the Fifties. It is hardly surprising that I have never gone to a meeting so full of apprehension. Would my hero – like so many others – have feet of clay? Worse, would he despise me as, I imagined, following his own experiences as a pupil and as a state school teacher (so hilariously revealed in this book), he must all members of my profession?

A. S. Neill was born in Forfar in 1883, and was educated in Kingsmuir Primary School by his father, the local dominie or teacher. The Scots word 'dominie' derives from the Latin *dominus*, meaning lord or master – which sums up the Scottish pupil-teacher relationships that Neill grew to abhor. His father conformed perfectly to the stereotype of a Scottish dominie; the curriculum was academic and the authoritarian regime enforced by the tawse, a heavy leather strap still used today to beat Scottish children. But his son was altogether a different matter. His early experiences had initiated Neill's lifelong search for a non-violent educational theory with the child's needs at the centre of attention, which reached its apotheosis at Summerhill between 1921 and 1973, the year of his death.

A Dominie's Log contains many of his later theories. Neill was in every way an oddity in Gretna Green, the Border village more famous for its passionate elopements, where the *Log* was written. He had returned to Scotland during the First World War, after a brief spell in London as a journalist. This experience – plus peculiar practices like summoning the pupils to school by bugle call (not good for the dignity, he acknowledges, and contemplates buying a cornet instead); or the use of the children's Christian names and his encouragement of their romantic fancies – set him at odds with the villagers who did not approve of his lax discipline or understand his informal approach. Although he was liked and befriended by many, the consensus was that he was, to use his own word, daft. This did not, however, prevent many parents attending a lecture,

'Children and their Parents', in the village hall, as we read in Chapter 14, when Neill attempted to tell the local townsfolk and farmers how to bring up their children, amid roars of laughter from all.

His great humour is evident throughout the *Log*, especially in his relationship with figures of authority, who are treated with much less respect than the pupils. Perhaps here are the beginnings of the democratic assemblies which became the hallmark of Summerhill in later years? In his outlook, his lifestyle and in his as yet undistilled theory of education, A. S. Neill was anything but the traditional dominie. His eccentricities were with him all his life but his theories concentrated into a heady new spirit that influenced education throughout the western world. In this exuberant book we see an atypical Scottish dominie and watch as his genuine love for young children develops into a struggle against corporal punishment, the examination system and a lack of resources in an Establishment school. Through the *Log* comes Neill's fascination with the vibrant young people of the village school and his attempts to develop a new curriculum, a curriculum which would not stultify his pupils' creativity but allow them an all too brief, but rich, experience to compensate for a bleak future in adult life.

He was acutely aware of the parochialism of country life and subscribed to the *New Statesman* and *New Age* to keep in contact with the wider world which was embroiled in the Great War and which filled him with such horror. Eventually these broader concerns took Neill south to exile, like many other Scots, to escape from claustrophobic village life and to allow his talents to flower. In London he came in contact with Homer Lane, his chief mentor, and Bertrand Russell, both leaders of the progressive educational movement who helped him shape the idiosyncratic version of a child-centred education which was later to become so closely identified with Summerhill.

In the early Twenties, Neill went to Austria to work in the International School at Hellorau, where he wrote *A Dominie Abroad*. Here, the intellectual challenge and fervour of the psychoanalytic movement excited him to such an extent that analysis was adopted at Summerhill. In 1937, during a lecture tour in Norway, he met Wilhelm Reich, a post-Freudian therapist who analysed Neill over a number of years. Their relationship developed into lifelong friendship, only terminating with Reich's death, in 1957, in an American jail during the McCarthy era. Late in his life Neill acknowledged his debt to psychoanalysis in general and Reich in particular, but claimed his own theory of education 'cured' more children than his therapy sessions ever did.

It is, perhaps, his early advocacy for the abolition of corporal punishment which has been of the greatest benefit to children, for the vast reduction of its use in schools in general, and primary schools in particular, is at least partly the result of Neill's influence. It is salutary to think that he was experimenting with abolition before the First World War, half a century before Strathclyde and Lothian education authorities, in his native Scotland, took the decision to ban corporal punishment. Even this step was only achieved after two Scottish parents took their abolitionist cause to the European Court of Justice. The court decision in 1982, in favour of the parents, will probably turn out to be a milestone in bringing about Neill's dream of a non-violent Scottish education system. It has been a long, hard struggle, by a growing band of educators working in the face of the educational establishment who had remained as devoted to corporal punishment as they were in Neill's day.

Rote learning, authoritarian classroom atmosphere and the examination system were some of the other horrors challenged by Neill in *A Dominie's Log* and throughout his long working life. His generosity and vivacity are a joy to all who read him. As an educationalist he was a man ahead of his time whose influence grew and spread before his death in 1973, both within the state school system and without. In his native Scotland, the only fee-paying offshoot of Summerhill is Kilquhanity House, in the south-west, run by James Aitkenhead following the philosophy of Neill and incorporating his democratic procedures. Teachers and parents disaffected with state education often actively sympathise with Neill's views – but there have been casualties. The dismissal of R. F. MacKenzie in 1974 from the headship of an Aberdeen school (ironically called Summerhill) after a bold experiment within the conventional system, is a clear example of the state headteacher being persecuted because of his attempt to follow Neill's progressive educational philosophy.

In fact, during my conversation with him that evening in the Fifties, Neill acknowledged the particular difficulties that face a state school teacher who wishes to follow the basic tenets of the progressive movement. This memory was helpful when, as had MacKenzie (no relation) in Aberdeen, I struggled to dispense with corporal punishment in Craigroyston and, in my attempt to make the classroom a more enjoyable place for the child to learn, discovered, like Neill, that noise was equated with indiscipline and its concomitant lack of learning. Like Neill, I have often felt at loggerheads with those elected representatives who were trying to achieve education 'on the cheap': he successfully exposed the lack of financial resources spent on education and had a highly ambivalent relationship with Her Majesty's Inspector of Schools. We are still fighting the same problems in education, though I admit that my own experiences with the Inspectorate are somewhat different. It was one of Her Majesty's Inspectors who paid Craigroyston High School its greatest compliment when he equated its atmosphere with that of Kilquhanity House. To be given this accolade was the high-water mark of my career, making me glad that I had managed to follow, to some extent, Neill's pioneering work in large state schools.

That night in Edinburgh was a great success. My apprehension was entirely unfounded, for meeting A. S. Neill was a marvellous experience. He was a man of genius, of warmth and affection, and, above all, a natural teacher.

Hugh D. MacKenzie, Edinburgh 1985

PREFACE.

THE first four instalments of this Log were published in the *Educational News*, under the acting editorship of Mr. Alexander Sivewright, who was very anxious to publish the Log in full, but apparently public opinion on the subject of the indiscriminate kissing of girls forced him to hold up the remainder.

Then teachers began to write me letters. Some of them were very complimentary; others weren't. These letters worried me, for I couldn't quite determine whether I was a lunatic or a genius. Then an unknown lady sent me a tract.

The title of the tract was : " The Sin That Found Him Out." The hero was a boy called Willie. He never told a lie, and when other boys smote him he turned the other cheek and prayed for them. " Life to him was one long prayer," said the tract. Then troubles came. He grew up and his father took to drink. His elder brother had a disagreement with

7

the local police about his whereabouts on the
night of a certain robbery, and was decidedly
unconvincing.   Willie stepped in and took all
the blame.

The next chapter takes Willie as a private
to the fields of Flanders, and the penultimate
chapter sees him a major-general.   The last
chapter contains the moral, but what the
moral is I cannot well make out.   In fact I
don't know whether the title refers to Willie
or his trangressing brother, but I feel that
somewhere in that pamphlet there is a lesson
for me.

Before the tract arrived I thought of pub-
lishing the Log as a brilliant treatise on
education.   Its arrival altered all my values.
I then knew that I was the educational
equivalent of the " awful example " who sits
on the platform at temperance meetings, and
with great humility I besought Mr. Herbert
Jenkins to publish my Log as a terrible warn-
ing to my fellow sinners.

A. S. N.

1915.

A DOMINIE'S LOG

AS A BOY I ATTENDED A VILLAGE
SCHOOL WHERE THE BAIRNS CHATTERED
AND WERE HAPPY. I TRACE MY LOVE
OF FREEDOM TO MY FREE LIFE THERE,
AND I DEDICATE THIS BOOK TO MY
FORMER DOMINIE, MY FATHER.

A DOMINIE'S LOG

I.

"NO reflections or opinions of a general character are to be entered in the log-book."—Thus the Scotch Code. I have resolved to keep a private log of my own. In the regulation volume I shall write down all the futile never-to-be-seen piffle about Mary Brown's being laid up with the measles, and about my anxiety lest it should spread. (Incidentally, my anxiety is real ; I do not want the school to be closed ; I want a summer holiday undocked of any days.) In my private log I shall write down my thoughts on education. I think they will be mostly original ; there has been no real authority on education, and I do not know of any book from which I can crib.

To-night after my bairns had gone away, I sat down on a desk and thought. What does it all mean ? What am I trying to do ? These boys are going out to the fields to plough ;

these girls are going to farms as servants. If I live long enough the new generation will be bringing notes of the plese-excuss-james-as-I-was-washing type....and the parents who will write them went out at that door five minutes ago. I can teach them to read, and they will read serials in the drivelling weeklies; I can teach them to write, and they will write pathetic notes to me by and bye; I can teach them to count, and they will never count more than the miserable sum they receive as a weekly wage. The " Three R's " spell futility.

But what of the rest ? Can I teach them drawing? I cannot. I can help a boy with a natural talent to improve his work, but of what avail is it ? In their future homes they will hang up the same old prints— vile things given away with a pound of tea. I can teach them to sing, but what will they sing ?....the *Tipperary* of their day.

My work is hopeless, for education should aim at bringing up a new generation that will be better than the old. The present system is to produce the same kind of man as we see to-day. And how hopeless he is. When first I saw Houndsditch, I said aloud : " We

have had education for generations....and
yet we have this." Yes, my work is hopeless. What is the use of the Three R's, of
Woodwork, of Drawing, of Geography, if
Houndsditch is to remain ? What is the
use of anything ?

* * *

I smile as I re-read the words I wrote
yesterday, for to-day I feel that hope has
not left me. But I am not any more hopeful
about the three R's and the others. I am
hopeful because I have found a solution. I
shall henceforth try to make my bairns
realise. Yes, realise is the word. Realise
what ? To tell the truth, I have some difficulty in saying. I think I want to make
them realise what life means. Yes, I want
to give them, or rather help them to find
an attitude. Most of the stuff I teach them
will be forgotten in a year or two, but an
attitude remains with one throughout life.
I want these boys and girls to acquire the
habit of looking honestly at life.

Ah ! I wonder if I look honestly at life
myself ! Am I not a very one-sided man ?
Am I not a Socialist, a doubter, a heretic ?
Am I not biassed when I judge men like the

Cecils and the Harmsworths ? I admit it. I am a partisan, and yet I try to look at life honestly. I try....and that is the main point. I do not think that I have any of the current superstitions about morality and religion and art. I try to forget names ; I try to get at essentials, at truth. The fathers of my bairns are, I think, interested in names. I wonder how many of them have sat down saying : " I must examine myself, so that I may find out what manner of man I am." I hold that self-knowledge must come before all things. When one has stripped off all the conventions, and superstitions, and hypocrisies, then one is educated.

*   *   *

These bairns of mine will never know how to find truth ; they will merely read the newspapers when they grow up. They will wave their hats to the King, but kingship will be but a word to them ; they will shout when a lawyer from the south wins the local seat, but they will not understand the meaning of economics ; they will dust their old silk hats and march to the sacrament, but they will not realise what religion means.

I find that I am becoming pessimistic again, and I did feel hopeful when I began to write. I *should* feel hopeful, for I am resolved to find another meaning in education. What was it ?....Ah, yes, I am to help them to find an attitude.

*   *   *

I have been thinking about discipline overnight. I have seen a headmaster who insisted on what he called perfect discipline. His bairns sat still all day. A movement foreshadowed the strap. Every child jumped up at the word of command. He had a very quiet life.

I must confess that I am an atrociously bad disciplinarian. To-day Violet Brown began to sing *Tipperary* to herself when I was marking the registers. I looked up and said : " Why the happiness this morning, Violet ? " and she blushed and grinned. I am a poor disciplinarian.

I find that normally I am very, very slack ; I don't mind if they talk or not. Indeed, if the hum of conversation stops, I feel that something has happened and I invariably look towards the door to see whether an Inspector has arrived.

I find that I am almost a good discip-linarian when my liver is bad; I demand silence then....but I fear I do not get it, and I generally laugh. The only discipline I ask for usually is the discipline that inte-rest draws. If a boy whets his pencil while I am describing the events that led to the Great Rebellion, I sidetrack him on the topic of rabbits....and I generally make him sit up. I know that I am teaching badly if the class is loafing, and I am honest enough in my saner moments not to blame the bairns.

I do not like strict discipline, for I do believe that a child should have as much freedom as possible. I want a bairn to be human, and I try to be human myself. I walk to school each morning with my briar between my lips, and if the fill is not smoked, I stand and watch the boys play. I would kiss my wife in my classroom, but....I do not have a wife. A wee lassie stopped me on the way to school this morning, and she pushed a very sticky sweetie into my hand. I took my pipe from my mouth and ate the sweetie— and I asked for another; she was highly delighted.

Discipline, to me, means a pose on the part of the teacher. It makes him very remote; it lends him dignity. Dignity is a thing I abominate. I suppose the bishop is dignified because he wants to show that there is a real difference between his salaried self and the underpaid curate. Why should I be dignified before my bairns? Will they scorn me if I slide with them? (There was a dandy slide on the road to-day. I gave them half-an-hour's extra play this morning, and I slid all the time. My assistants are adepts at the game.)

But discipline is necessary; there are men known as Inspectors. And Johnny must be flogged if he does not attend to the lesson. He must know the rivers of Russia. After all, why should he? I don't know them, and I don't miss the knowledge. I couldn't tell you the capital of New Zealand....is it Wellington? or Auckland? I don't know; all I know is that I could find out if I wanted to.

I do not blame Inspectors. Some of them are men with what I would call a vision. I had the Chief Inspector of the district in the other day, and I enjoyed his visit. He has a fine taste in poetry, and a sense of humour.

The Scotch Education Department is iniquitous because it is a department; a department cannot have a sense of humour. And it is humour that makes a man decent and kind and human.

If the Scotch Education Department were to die suddenly I should suddenly become a worse disciplinarian than I am now. If Willie did not like Woodwork, I should say to him: " All right, Willie. Go and do what you do like, but take my advice and do some work; you will enjoy your football all the better for it."

I believe in discipline, but it is self-discipline that I believe in. I think I can say that I never learned anything by being forced to learn it, but I may be wrong. I was forced to learn the Shorter Catechism, and to-day I hate the sight of it. I read the other day in Barrie's *Sentimental Tommy* that its meaning comes to one long afterwards and at a time when one is most in need of it. I confess that the time has not come for me; it will never come, for I don't remember two lines of the Catechism.

It is a fallacy that the nastiest medicines are the most efficacious; Epsom Salts are not more beneficial than Syrup of Figs.

A thought!....If I believe in self-discipline, why not persuade Willie that Woodwork is good for him as a self-discipline? Because it isn't my job. If Willie dislikes chisels he will always dislike them. What I might do is this : tell him to persevere with his chisels so that he might cut himself badly. Then he might discover that his true vocation is bandaging, and straightway go in for medicine.

Would Willie run away and play at horses if I told him to do what he liked best? I do not think so. He likes school, and I think he likes me. I think he would try to please me if he could.

* * *

When I speak kindly to a bairn I sometimes ask myself what I mean (for I try to find out my motives). Do I want the child to think kindly of me? Do I try to be popular? Am I after the delightful joy of being loved? Am I merely being humanly brotherly and kind?

I have tried to analyse my motives, and I

really think that there is little of each motive.
I want to be loved; I want the bairn to
think kindly of me. But in the main I
think that my chief desire is to make the
bairn happy. No man, no woman, has the
right to make the skies cloudy for a bairn;
it is the sin against the Holy Ghost.

I once had an experience in teaching. A
boy was dour and unlovable and rebellious
and disobedient. I tried all ways—I regret
to say I tried the tawse. I was inexperienced
at the time yet I hit upon the right way.
One day I found he had a decided talent for
drawing. I brought down some of my pen-
and-ink sketches and showed him them. I
gave him pictures to copy, and his interest
in art grew. I won him over by interesting
myself in him. He discovered that I was
only human after all.

Only human !....when our scholars discover that we are only human, then they
like us, and then they listen to us.

I see the fingers of my tawse hanging out
of my desk. They seem to be two accusing
fingers. My ideals are all right, but....I
whacked Tom Wilkie to-night. At three
o'clock he bled Dave Tosh's nose, and because

Dave was the smaller, I whacked Tom. Yet I did not feel angry; I regret to say that I whacked Tom because I could see that Dave expected me to do it, and I hate to disappoint a bairn. If Dave had been his size, I know that I should have ignored their battle.

*   *   *

I have not used the strap all this week, and if my liver keeps well, I hope to abolish it altogether.

To-day I have been thinking about punishment. What is the idea of punishment? A few months ago a poor devil of an engine-driver ran his express into a goods, and half-a-dozen people were killed. He got nine months. Why? Is his punishment meant to act as a deterrent? Will another driver say to himself: "By Jove, I'll better not wreck my train or I'll get nine months." Nine months is not punishment, but the life-long thought : " I did it," is hell.

I am trying to think why I punished Lizzie Smith for talking last Friday. Bad habit, I expect. Yet it acted as a deterrent; it showed that I was in earnest about what I was saying—I was reading the war news from the *Scotsman*.

I am sorry that I punished her; it was weakness on my part, weakness and irritation. If she had no interest in the war, why should she pretend that she had? But no, I cannot have this. I must inculcate the idea of a community; the bairn must be told that others have rights. I often want to rise up and contradict the minister in kirk, but I don't; the people have rights; they do not come out to listen to me. If I offend against the community, the community will punish me with ostracism or bitterness. We have all a right to live our own lives, but in living them we must live in harmony with the community. Lizzie must be told that all the others like the war news, and that in talking she is annoying them. Yes, I must remember to emphasise continually the idea of a corporate life.

*   *   *

I see that it is only the weak man who requires a strap. Lord Kitchener could rule my school without a strap, but I am not Kitchener. Moreover, I am glad I'm not. I do not want to be what is called a strong man. John Gourlay, in *The House with the Green Shutters* was strong enough to rule every school in Scotland with Sir John Struthers superadded ; yet I do not want to be Gourlay. His son would have been a better teacher, for he was more human. Possibly Kitchener is very human ; I do not know.

1f.

I HEARD a blackie this morning as I went
to school, and when I came near to the
playground I heard the girls singing.
And I realised that Lenten was come with
love to Town.

The game was a jingaring, and Violet
Brown was in the centre.

> The wind and the wind and the wind blows high,
> The rain comes pattering from the sky.
> Violet Brown says she 'll die
> For the lad with the rolling eye.
> She is handsome, she is pretty,
> She is the girl of the golden city;
> She is counted one, two, three,
> Oh ! I wonder who he 'll be.
> Willie Craig says he loves her......

My own early experiences told me that Willie
wasn't far off. Yes, there he was at the same
old game. When Vi entered the ring Willie
began to hammer Geordie Steel with his
bonnet. But I could see Violet watch him with
a corner of her eye, and I am quite sure that
she was aware that the exertion of hammering
Geordie did not account for Willie's burning
cheeks.

Then Katie Farmer entered the ring.... and Tom Dixon at once became the hammerer of Geordie.

Poor wee Geordie! I know that he loves Katie himself, and I know that between blows he is listening for the fatal "Tom Dixon says he loves her."

I re-arranged seats this morning, and Willie is now sitting behind his Vi, but Tom Dixon is not behind Katie. Poor despised Geordie is there, but I shall shift him to-morrow if he does not make the most of his chances.

* * *

This morning Geordie passed a note over to Katie, then he sat all in a tremble. I saw Katie read it....and I saw her blush. I blew my nose violently, for I knew what was written on that sacred sheet; at least I thought I knew...." Dear Katie, will you be my lass? I will have you if you will have me—Geordie."

At minutes I listened for the name when Katie went into the ring. It was "Tom Dixon" again. I blew my whistle and stopped the game.

At dinner-time I looked out at the window, and rejoiced to see poor Geordie hammering

Tom Dixon. I opened the window and listened. Katie was in the ring again, and I almost shouted " Hurrah ! " when I heard the words, " Geordie Steel says he loves her." But I placed Tom Dixon behind Katie in the afternoon ; I felt that I had treated poor Tom with injustice.

To-night I tried to tackle Form 9b, but I could not concentrate. But it wasn't Violet and Katie that I was thinking of ; I was thinking of the Violets and Katies I wrote " noties " to many years ago. I fear I am a bit of a sentimentalist, yet....why the devil shouldn't I be ?

*   *   *

I have discovered a girl with a sense of humour. I asked my Qualifying Class to draw a graph of the attendance at a village kirk. " And you must explain away any rise or fall," I said.

Margaret Steel had a huge drop one Sunday, and her explanation was " Special Collection for Missions." Next Sunday the congregation was abnormally large ; Margaret wrote " Change of Minister."

Few bairns have a sense of humour ; their's is a sense of fun. Make a noise like a duck and they will scream, but tell them your best joke and they will be bored to tears.

I try hard to cultivate their sense of humour and their imagination. In their composition I give them many autobiographies.. ....a tile hat, a penny, an old boot, a nose, a tooth. To-day I asked them to describe in the first person a snail's journey to the end of the road. Margaret Steel talked of her hundred mile crawl, and she noted the tall forests on each side of the road. " The grass would be trees to a snail," she explained.

Poor Margaret ! When she is fourteen she will go out to the fields, and in three years she will be an ignorant country bumpkin. Our education system is futile because it does not go far enough. The State should see to it that each child has the best of chances. Margaret should be sent to a Secondary School and to a University free of charge. Her food and clothes and books and train fares should be free by right. The lassie has brains....and that is argument enough.

Our rulers do realize to a slight extent the responsibility of the community to the child. It sends a doctor round to look at Margaret's teeth ; it may feed her at school if she is starving ; it compels her to go to school till she is fourteen. At the age of fourteen she is free to go to the devil—the factory or the herding.

But suppose she did go to a Secondary School. What then ? Possibly she would become a Junior Student or a University Student. She would learn much, but would she think ? I found that thinking was not encouraged at the university.

*   *   *

To-day I asked Senior I. to write up " A hen in the Kirk," and one or two attempts showed imagination.

Is it possible that I am overdoing the imagination business ? Shall I produce men and women with more imagination than intellect ? No, I do not think there is danger. The nation suffers from lack of imagination ; few of us can imagine a better state of society, a fuller life.

Who are the men with great imagination ? ....Shelley, Blake, Browning, Nietzsche, Ibsen, Tolstoy. These men were not content with life as it was ; they had ideals, and ideals are creatures of the imagination.

I once saw a book by, I think, Arnold
Forster; a book that was meant to teach
children the meaning of citizenship. If I
remember aright it dealt with parliament and
law, and local government.

Who was Arnold Forster? Why cannot
our bairns have the best? Why tell them
all the stale lies about democracy, the freedom of the individual, the justice of our
laws? Are Forster's ideas of citizenship as
great as the ideas of Plato, of More, of Morris,
of Wells? I intend to make an abridgement
of Plato's *Republic*, More's *Utopia*, William
Morris's *News from Nowhere*, Bacon's *A New
Atlantis*, H. G. Wells' *A Modern Utopia*, and
New Worlds for Old.

Arnold Forster was with the majority.
Nearly every day I quote to my bairns
Ibsen's words from *An Enemy of the People*.
...."The Majority *never* has right on its
side. *Never* I say." Every lesson book
shouts aloud the words: "The majority is
always right."

Do I teach my bairns Socialism? I do
not think so. Socialism means the owning
of a State by the people of that State, and
this State is not fit to own anything. For at

present the State means the majority in
Parliament, and that is composed of medi-
ocre men. A State that takes up Home
Rule while the slums of the East End exist
is a State run by office boys for office boys....
to adapt Salisbury's description of a London
daily. We could not have Socialism to-day ;
the nation is not ripe for it.

The Germans used to drink to " The Day " ;
every teacher in Britain should drink daily
to " The Day " when there shall be no poor,
when factory lasses will not rise at five and
work till six. I know that I shall never see
the day, but I shall tell my bairns that it is
coming. I know that most of the seed will
fall on stony ground, but a sower can but
sow.

*　　*　　*

I have been image-breaking to-day, and 1
feel happy. It began with patent medicines,
but how I got to them I cannot recollect.
I remember commencing a lesson on George
Washington. The word hatchet led naturally to Women's Suffrage ; then ducks came
up....Heaven only knows how, and the
word quack brought me to Beans for Bibulous
Britons. I told how most of these medicines

cost half a farthing to make, and I explained that the manufacturer was spending a good part of the shilling profit in advertising. Then I told of the utter waste of material and energy in advertising, and went on to thunder against the hideous yellow tyre signs on the roadside.

At dinner-time I read in my paper that some knight had received his knighthood because of his interest in the Territorial Movement. " Much more likely that he gave a few thousands to the party funds," I said to my wondering bairns. Then I cursed the cash values that attach to almost everything.

I am determined to tear all the rags of hypocrisy from the facts of life ; I shall lead my bairns to doubt everything. Yet I want them to believe in Peter Pan, or is it that I want them to believe in the beauty of beautiful stories ? I want them to love the alluring lady Romance, but I think I want them to love her in the knowledge that she is only a Dream Child. Romance means more to the realist than to the romancist.

* * *

I wish I were a musician. If I could play

the piano I should spend each Friday afternoon playing to my bairns. I should give
them Alexander's Ragtime Band and Hitchy
Coo; then I should play them a Liszt Rhapsody and a Chopin waltz.

Would they understand and appreciate?
Who knows what raptures great music might
bring to a country child?

The village blacksmith was fiddling at a
dance in the Hall last night. "Aw learnt
the fiddle in a week," he told me. I believed
him.

What effect would Ysaye have on a village
audience? The divine melody would make
them sit up startled at first, and, I think,
some of them might begin to see pictures.
If only I could bring Ysaye and Pachmann
to this village! What an experiment! I
think that if I were a Melba or a Ysaye I
should say to myself:—" I have had enough
of money and admiration; I shall go round
the villages on an errand of mercy."

The great, they say, begin in the village
hall and end in the Albert Hall. The really
great would begin and end in the village hall.

III.

A VERY young calf had managed to get into the playground this morning, and when I arrived I found Peter Smith hitting it viciously over the nose with a stick. I said nothing. I read the war news as usual. Then I addressed the bairns.

" What would you do to the Germans who committed atrocities in Belgium ? " I asked. Peter's hand went up with the others.

" Well, Peter ? "

" Please sir, shoot them."

" Cruelty should be punished, eh ? " I said.

" Yes, sir."

" Then come here, you dirty dog ! " I cried, and I whacked Peter with a fierce joy.

I have often wondered at the strain of cruelty that is so often found in boys. The evolutionists must be right : the young always tend to resemble their remote ancestors. In a boy there is much of the brute.

I have seen a boy cut off the heads of a nest
of young sparrows ; I wanted to hit him. . . .
but he was bigger than I. This morning I
was bigger than Peter ; hence I do not take
any credit to myself for welting him.

I can see that cruelty does not disappear
with youth. I confess to a feeling of unholy
joy in leathering Peter, but I think that it
was caused by a real indignation.

What made Peter hurt the poor wee thing
I cannot tell. I am inclined to think that
he acted subconsciously ; he was being the
elemental hunter, and he did not realise that
he was giving pain. I ought to have talked
to him, to have made him realise. But I
became elemental also ; I punished with no
definite motive. . . . and I would do it again.

*   *   *

We have had a return of wintry weather,
and the bairns had a glorious slide made on
the road this morning. At dinner-time I
found them loafing round the door.

" Why aren't you sliding," I asked. They
explained that the village policeman had
salted the slide. After marking the registers
I took up the theme.

" Why did he salt the slide ? " I asked.

" Because the farmers do not want their horses to fall," said one.

Then I took them to laws and their makers. " Children have no votes," I said, " farmers have; hence the law is with the farmers. Women have no votes and the law gives them half the salary of a man."

" But," said Margaret Steel, " would you have horses break their legs ? " I smiled.

" No," I said, " and I would not object to the policeman's salting the slide if the law was thinking of animals' pain. The law and the farmers are thinking of property.

" Property in Britain comes before everything. I may steal the life and soul from a woman if I employ her at a penny an hour, and I may get a title for doing so. But if I steal Mr. Thomson's turnips I merely get ten days' hard."

" You bairns should draw up a Declaration of Rights," I added, and I think that a few understood my meaning.

* * *

I find that my bairns have a genuine love for poetry. To-day I read them Tennyson's *Lady of Shalott;* then I read them *The May Queen.* I asked them which was the better,

and most of them preferred, *The Lady of
Shalott.* I asked for reasons, and Margaret
Steel said that the one was strange and
mysterious, while the other told of an ordinary
death-bed. The whole class seemed to be
delighted when I called *The May Queen* a
silly mawkish piece of sentimentality.

I have made them learn many pieces from
Stevenson's *A Child's Garden of Verses,* and
they love the rhythm of such pieces as *The
Shadow March.*

Another poem that they love is *Helen
of Kirkconnell;* I asked which stanza
was the best, and they all agreed on this
beautifully simple one :—

> O Helen fair, beyond compare,
>   I'll mak a garland o' thy hair ;
> Shall bind my heart for evermair,
>   Until the day I dee,

I believe in reading out a long poem and
then asking them to memorise a few verses.
I did this with *The Ancient Mariner.* Long
poems are an abomination to children ; to
ask them to commit to memory a piece like
Gray's *Elegy* is unkind.

I have given them the first verse of Francis
Thompson's *The Hound of Heaven.* I did
not expect them to understand a word of it ;

my idea was to test their power of appreciating sound. Great music might convey something to rustics, but great poetry cannot convey much. Still, I try to lead them to the greater poetry. I wrote on the board a verse of *Little Jim* and a verse of *La Belle Dame sans Merci*, and I think I managed to give them an inkling of what is good and what is bad verse.

I begin to think that country children should learn ballads. There is a beauty about the old ballads that even children can catch ; it is the beauty of a sweet simplicity. When I think of the orchestration of Swinburne, I think of the music of the ballads as of a flute playing. And I know that orchestration would be lost on country folk.

I hate the poems that crowd the average school-book....*Little Jim*, *We are Seven*, *Lucy Gray*, *The Wreck of the Hesperus*, *The Boy stood on the Burning Deck*, and all the rest of them. I want to select the best of the Cavalier lyrists' works, the songs from the old collections like Davison's *Poetical Rhapsody* and *England's Helicon*, the lyrics from the Elizabethan dramatists. I want to look through moderns like William Watson,

Robert Bridges, George Meredith, Thomas Hardy, Henley, Dowson, Abercrombie, William Wilfred Gibson....there must be many charming pieces that bairns would enjoy.

I read out the old *Tale of Gamelyn* the other day, and the queer rhythm and language seemed to interest the class.

* * *

I think that the teaching of history in schools is all wrong. I look through a school-history, and I find that emphasis is laid on incident. Of what earthly use is the information given about Henry VIII.'s matrimonial vagaries? Does it matter a rap to anyone whether Henry I.— or was it Henry II.?—ever smiled again or not? By all means let us tell the younger children tales of wicked dukes, but older children ought to be led to think out the meaning of history. The usual school-history is a piece of snobbery; it can't keep away from the topic of kings and queens. They don't matter; history should tell the story of the people and their gradual progress from serfdom to......sweating.

I believe that a boy of eleven can grasp cause and effect. With a little effort he can

understand the non-sentimental side ot the
Mary Stewart-Elizabeth story, the result to
Scotland of the Franco-Scottish alliance. He
can understand why Philip of Spain, a Roman
Catholic, preferred that the Protestant Eliza-
beth should be Queen of England rather than
the Catholic Mary Stewart.

The histories never make bairns think.
I have not seen one that mentioned that
Magna Charta was signed because all classes
in the country happened to be united for
the moment. I have not seen one that
points out that the main feature in Scots
history is the lack of a strong central government.

Hume Brown's school *History of Scotland*
is undoubtedly a very good book, but I want
to see a history that will leave out all the
detail that Brown gives. All that stuff about
the Ruthven Raid and the Black Dinner of
the Douglases might be left out of the books
that the upper classes read. My history
would tell the story of how the different parts
were united to form the present Scotland,
without mentioning more than half-a-dozen
names of men and dates. Then it would go
on to tell of the struggles to form a central

government. Possibly Hume Brown does this. 1 don't know ; I am met with so much detail about Perth Articles and murders that I lose the thread of the story.

Again, the school-histories almost always give a wrong impression of men and events. Every Scots schoolboy thinks that Edward I. of England was a sort of thief and bully rolled into one, and that the carpet-bagger, Robert Bruce, was a saint from heaven. Edward's greatness as a lawgiver is ignored ; at least we ought to give him credit for his statesmanship in making an attempt to unite England, Scotland, and Wales. And Cromwell's Drogheda and Wexford affair is generally mentioned with due emphasis, while Charles I.'s proverbial reputation as " a bad king but a good father " is seldom omitted.

I expect that the school-histories of the future will talk of the " scrap of paper " aspect of the present war, and they will anathematise the Kaiser. But the real historians will be searching for deeper causes ; they will be analysing the national characteristics, the economical needs, the diplomatic methods, of the nations.

The school-histories will say : " The war

came about because the Kaiser wanted to be master of Europe, and the German people had no say in the matter at all."

The historians will say....well, I'm afraid I don't know ; but I think they will relegate the Kaiser to a foot-note.

*   *   *

The theorist is a lazy man. MacMurray down the road at Markiton School is a hard worker ; he never theorises about education. He grinds away at his history and geography, and I don't suppose he likes geography any more than I do. I expect that he gives a thorough lesson on Canada, its exports and so on. I do not ; I am too lazy to read up the subject. My theory says to me : " You are able to think fairly well, and a knowledge of the amount of square miles in Manitoba would not help you to think as brightly as H. G. Wells. So, why learn up stuff that you can get in a dictionary any day ? " And I teach on this principle.

At the same time I am aware that facts must precede theories in education. You cannot have a theory on, say, the Marriage Laws, unless you know what these laws are. However, I do try to distinguish between facts and facts. To a child (as to me), the fact that Canada grows wheat is of less importance than the fact that if you walk down the street in Winnipeg in mid winter, you may have your ears frost-bitten.

The only information I know about Japan consists of a few interesting facts I got from a lecture by Arthur Diosy. I don't know what things are manufactured in Tokio, but I know that a Jap almost boils himself when he takes a bath in the morning.

I find that I am much more interested in humanity than in materials, and I know that the bairns are like me in this.

A West African came to the school the other day, and asked me to allow him to tell (for a consideration) the story of his home life. When I discovered that he did not mean his own private home life I gladly gave him permission. He talked for half-an-hour about the habits of his home, the native schools, the dress of the children (I almost blushed at this part, but I was relieved to find that they do dress after all) ; then he sang the native version of ' Mary had a little Lamb ' (great applause).

The lecture was first-rate ; and, in my lazy

—I mean my theoretical moments, I squint down the road in hopes that an itinerant Chinaman will come along. I would have a coloured band of geographers employed by the Department.

*   *   *

I am chuckling at myself to-night. A day or two ago I lectured about the policeman's action in salting the slide, and I certainly did not think of the farmer's position. To-day I wore a new pair of very light spats... and Lizzie Adam has a horrid habit of shaking her pen after dipping.

"Look what you've done!" I cried in vexation, "can't you stop that silly habit of chucking ink all over the school?" Then I laughed.

"Lizzie," I said sadly, "you won't understand, but I am the farmer who wants the slide salted. The farmer does not want to have his horse ruined, and I do object to having my new spats ruined."

The truth is that the interests of the young and of the old are directly antagonistical. I can argue with delightful sophistry that I am better than the farmer. I can say that throwing ink is a silly habit, with no benefit

to Lizzie, while sliding brings joy to a school-
ful of bairns ; hence the joy of these bairns
is of greater importance than the loss of a
horse.   But I know what I should think
if it were my horse, yes, I know.

I find it the most difficult thing in the world
to be a theorist . . . . and an honest
man at the same time.

IV.

A JUNIOR Inspector called to-day His subject was handwriting, and he had theories on the subject. So have I. We had an interesting talk.

His view is that handwriting is a practical science ; hence we must teach a child to write in such a way as to carry off the job he applies for when he is fourteen.

My view is that handwriting is an art, like sketching My view is the better, for it includes his. I am a superior penman to him, and in a contest I could easily beat him. I really failed to see what he was worrying his head about. What does the style matter. It is the art that one puts into a style that makes writing good. I can teach the average bairn to write well in two hours ; it is simply a matter of writing slowly I like the old-schoolmaster hand, the round easy writing with its thick downstrokes and thin upstrokes. I like to see the m's with the joinings in the middle. The *Times* copy-book is the ideal

one—to me.   But why write down any more.
The topic isn't worth the ink wasted.

*   *   *

I picked up a copy of a Popular Educator
to-day.   Much of the stuff seems to be well
written, but I cannot help thinking that the
words " low ideals" are written over the whole
set of volumes.   Its aim is evidently to
enable boys and girls to gain success   . . .
as the world considers success.   " Study hard,"
it blares forth, " and you will become a White-
ley or a Gamage.   Study if you want wealth
and position."   What an ideal !

Let us have our Shorthand Classes, our
Cookery Classes, our Typewriting Classes,
but for any sake don't let us call them education.   Education is thinking ; it should deal
with great thoughts, with the æsthetic things
in life, with life itself.   Commerce is the
profiteer's god, but it is not mine.   I
want to teach my bairns how to live ;
the Popular Educator wants to teach them
how to make a living.   There is a distinction
between the two ideals.

The Scotch Education Department would
seem to have some of the Educator's aspira-
tions.   It demands Gardening, Woodwork,

Cookery ; in short, it is aiming at turning out practical men and women.

My objection to men and women is that they are too practical. I used to see a notice in Edinburgh : " John Brown, Practical Chimney Sweep." I often used to wonder what a theoretical chimney sweep might be, and I often wished I could meet one. My view is that a teacher should turn out theoretical sweeps, railwaymen, ploughmen, servants. Heaven knows they will get the practical part knocked into them soon enough.

*   *   *

I have been experimenting with Drawing. I have been a passable black-and-white artist for many years, and the subject fascinates me. I see that drawing is of less importance than taste, and I find that I can get infants who cannot draw a line to make artistic pictures.

I commence with far-away objects—a clump of trees on the horizon. The child takes a BB pencil and blocks in the mass of trees. The result is a better picture than the calendar prints the bairns see at home.

Gradually I take nearer objects, and at length I reach what is called drawing. I

ignore all vases and cubes and ellipses ; my
model is a school-bag or a cloak.   The drawing
does not matter very much ; but I want to
see the shadows stand out.

I find that only a few in a class ever improve
in sketching ; one is born with the gift.

Designing fascinates many bairns.   I asked
them to design a kirk window on squared
paper to-day.   Some of the attempts were
good.   I got the boys to finish off with red
ink, and then I pasted up the designs on the
wall.

I seem to recollect an Inspector who told
me to give up design a good few years ago.
I wouldn't give it up now for anyone.   It is a
delightful study, and it will bring out an
inherent good taste better than any branch
of drawing I know.   Drawing (or rather,
Sketching) to me means an art, not a means
to cultivating observation.   It belongs solely
to Aesthetics.   Sketching, Music, and Poetry
are surely intended to make a bairn realise
the fuller life that must have beauty always
with it.

I showed my bairns two sketches of my
own to-day. . .   the Tolbooth and the
Whitehorse Close in Edinburgh.   A few

claimed that the Whitehorse Close was the better, because it left more out. " It leaves something to the imagination," said Tom Dixon.

*　　*　　*

When will some original publisher give us a decent school Reader ? I have not seen one that is worth using. Some of them give excerpts from Dickens and Fielding and Borrow (that horrid bore) and Hawthorne (another). I cannot find any interest in these excerpts ; they have no beginning and no end. Moreover, a bairn does like the dramatic; prosiness deadens its wee soul at once.

I want to see a Reader especially written for bairns. I want to see many complete stories, filled with bright dialogue. Every yarn should commence with dialogue. I always think kindly of the late Guy Boothby, because he usually began with, " Hands up, or I fire ! " or a kindred sentence.

I wish I could lay hands on a Century Reader I used as a boy. It was full of the dramatic. The first story was one about the Burning of Moscow, then came the tale of Captain Dodds and the pirate (from

Reade's novel, *Hard Cash*, I admit. An excerpt need not be uninteresting), then a long passage from *The Deerslayer* ....with a picture of Indians throwing tomahawks at the hero. I loved that book.

I think that dramatic reading should precede prosy reading. It is life that a child wants, not prosy descriptions of sunsets and travels ; life, and romance.

I have scrapped my Readers; I don't use them even for Spelling. I do not teach Spelling ; the teaching of it does not fit into my scheme of education.

Teaching depends on logic. Now Spelling throws logic to the winds. I tell a child that " cough " is " coff," and logic leads him to suppose that rough is " roff " and " through " is " throff." If I tell him that spelling is important because it shows whence a word is derived, I am bound in honesty to tell him that a matinee is not a " morning performance," that manufactured goods are not " made by hand." Hence I leave Spelling alone.

At school I " learned " Spelling, and I could not spell a word until I commenced to read much. Spelling is of the eye mainly.

Every boy can spell " truly " and " obliged "
when he leaves school, but ten years later he
will probably write " truely " and " oblidged."
Why ?   I think that the explanation lies
in the fact that he does not read as a growing
youth.   Anyway, dictionaries are cheap.

*   *   *

To-night I sat down on a desk and lit my
pipe. Margaret Steel and Lizzie Buchan
were tidying up the room. Margaret looked
at me thoughtfully for a second.

" Please, sir, why do you smoke ? " she
said.

" I really don't know, Margaret," I said.
" Bad habit, I suppose....just like writing
notes to boys."

She suddenly became feverishly anxious
to pick up the stray papers.

" I wonder," I mused, " whether they do
it in the same old way. How do they do it,
Margaret ? " She dived after a piece of
paper.

" I used to write them myself," I said.
Margaret looked up quickly.

" You ! " she gasped.

" I am not so old," I said hastily.

" Please, sir, I didn't mean that," she explained in confusion.

" You did, you wee bissom," I chuckled.

" Please, sir," she said awkwardly, " why—why are you not—not–m–married ? " I rose and took up my hat.

" I once kissed a girl behind the school door, Margaret," I said absently. She did not understand....and when I come to think of it I am not surprised.

*   *   *

To-day was prize-giving day. Old Mr. Simpson made a speech.

" Boys," he said, " study hard and you'll maybe be a minister like Mr. Gordon there." He paused. " Or," he continued, " if you don't manage that, you may become a teacher like Mr. Neill here."

Otherwise the affair was very pathetic : the medallist, a girl, had already left school and was hired as a servant on a farm. And old Mr. Simpson did not know it ; I thought it better not to tell the kindly soul. He spoke earnestly on success in life.

I hate prizes. To-day, Violet Brown and Margaret Steel, usually the best of friends, are looking daggers at each other. Tomorrow I shall read them the story of the Judgment of Paris. And what rubbish these books are! There isn't a decent piece of literature in the bunch. -*Matty's Present, The Girl Who Came to School.* Jerusalem!

V.

THE more I see of it the more I admire the co-education system. To me it is delightful to see boys and girls playing together. Segregate boys and you destroy their perspective. I used to find at the university that it was generally the English Public School Boy who set up one standard of morals for his sisters and another for the shop-girls.

Co-education is the greatest thing in our State educational system. The bairns early learn the interdependence of the sexes ; boys and girls early begin to understand each other. All danger of putting women on a pedestal is taken away ; the boys find that the girls are ordinary humans with many failings ("Aw'll tell the mester ! "), and many virtues. The girls find that boys....well, I don't exactly know what the girls find.

Seldom is there any over-familiarity. The girls have a natural protective aloofness that awes the boys ; the boys generally have

strenuous interests that lead them to ignore
the girls for long periods. At present the
sexes are very friendly, for love-making
(always a holy thing with bairns), has come
with spring ; but in a few weeks the boys will
be playing football or " bools," and they will
not be seen in the girls' playground.

I can detect no striving after what is called
chivalry (thank heaven !) If Maggie and
Willie both lay hands on a ruler, they fight it
out, but Maggie generally gets it ; she can
say more. Mr. Henpeck begins life as a
chick. I hate the popular idea of chivalry,
and I want my boys to hate it. Chivalry to
me means rising in the Tube to offer a typist
your seat, and then going off to the city to
boss a score of waitresses who are paid 6s.
a week. As a nation we have no chivalry ; we
have only etiquette. We hold doors open
for nice women, and we tamely suffer or
forget about a society that condemns poor
women to slave for sixteen hours a day sewing
shirts at a penny an hour. We say " Thank
you" when the lady of the house stops playing,
and we banish the prostitutes of Piccadilly
from our minds. Chivalry has been dead
for a long time now.

I want to substitute kindness for the word chivalry. I want to tell my bairns that the only sin in the world is cruelty. I do not preach morality for I hardly know what morality is. I have no morals, I am an a-moralist, or should it be a non-moralist ? I judge not, and I mean to school my bairns into judging not. Yet I am not being quite consistent. I do judge cruelty and uncharitableness ; but I judge not those who do not act up to the accustomed code of morals. A code is always a temptation to a healthy person ; it is like a window by a railway siding : it cries out : " Chuck a chunk of coal through me." Codes never make people moral; they merely make them hypocritical. I include the Scotch code.

*   *   *

Until lately I thought that drill was unnecessary for rural bairns. It was the chief inspector of the district who converted me. He pointed out that country children are clumsy and slack. " A countryman can heave a sack of potatoes on his back," he said, " but he has no agility, no grace of movement."

I agree with him now. I find that drill makes my bairns more graceful. But I am far from being pleased with any system that I know. I don't really care tuppence whether they are physically alert or not, but I want them to be graceful, if only from an artistic point of view. The system I really want to know is Eurhythmics. I recently read an illustrated article by (or on ?) Jacques Dalcroze, the inventor of the method, and the founder of the Eurhythmics School near Dresden. The system is drill combined with music. The pupils walk and dance, and I expect, sit to music. The photographs were beautiful studies in grace ; the school appears to be full of Pavlovas. I think I shall try to found a Eurhythmics system on the photographs. I cannot surely invent anything more graceless than " 'Shun ! "

Grace is almost totally absent from rural dances. The ploughman takes off his jacket, and sweats his roaring way through " The Flowers o' Edinburgh " ; but the waltz has no attraction for him. Waltzing is a necessity in a rural scheme of education....and, incidentally, in a Mayfair scheme of education, now that the " Bunny Hug " and the " Turkey

Trot " and the " Tango " have come to these
isles.

*   *   *

Robert Campbell left the school to-day.
He had reached the age limit. He begins
work tomorrow morning as a ploughman.
And yesterday I wrote about introducing
Eurhythmics ! Robert's leaving brings me
to earth with a flop. I am forced to look a
grim fact in the face. Truly it is like a
death ; I stand by a new made grave, and I
have no hope of a resurrection. Robert is dead.

Pessimism has hold of me to-night. I
have tried to point the way to what I think
best in life, tried to give Robert an ideal.
Tomorrow he will be gathered to his fathers.
He will take up the attitude of his neighbours :
he will go to church, he will vote Radical or
Tory, he will elect a farmer to the School
Board, he will marry and live in a hovel. His
master said to me recently : " Bairns are
gettin' ower muckle eddication noo-a-days.
What eddication does a laddie need to herd
kye ? "

Yes, 1 am as pessimistic as any Schopen-
hauer to-night, I cannot see the sun.

*   *   *

My pessimism has remained with me all day. I feel that I am merely pouring water into a sieve. I almost feel that to meddle with education is to begin at the wrong end. I may have an ideal, but I cannot carry it out because I am up against all the forces of society. Robert Campbell is damned, not because education is so very wrong, but because education is trying to adapt itself to commerce and economics and convention. I think I am right in holding that our Individualist, as opposed to a Socialist, system is to blame. "Every man for himself" is the most cursed saying that was ever said. If we are to allow an idle rich to waste millions yearly, if we are to allow profiteers to amass thousands at the expense of the slaving majority, what chance has poor Robert Campbell? I complete the saying—" and the Deil tak the henmost." Robert is the henmost.

O! the people are poor things. Democracy is the last futility. Yet I should not blame the people ; they never get a chance. Our rulers are on the side of the profiteers, and the latter take very good care that Robert Campbell shall leave school when he is fourteen. It isn't that they want more cheap labour ; they are afraid that if he is educated until he is nineteen he will be wise enough to say : " Why should I, a man made in the image of God, be forced to slave for gains that you will steal ? "

Yet, the only way is to labour on, to strive to convey some idea of my ideal to my bairns. If every teacher in Scotland had the same ideal as I have I think that the fight would not be a long one. But how do I know that my ideal is the right one ? I cannot say ; I just *know*. Which, I admit, is a woman's reason.

*   *   *

I was re-reading *An Enemy of the People* last night, and the thought suddenly came to me : " Would my bairns understand it ? " This morning I cut out Bible instruction and read them the first act. I then questioned them, and found to my delight that they had grasped the theme. It was peculiarly satisfying to me to find that they recognized Dr. Stockmann as a better man than his grovelling brother Peter. If my bairns could realise the full significance of Ibsen's play, " The

Day " would not be so far off as I am in the habit of thinking it is.

I must re-read Shaw's *Widowers' Houses* ; I fancy that children might find much thought in it. It is one of his " Unpleasant Plays," but I see no reason for keeping the unlovely things from bairns. I do not believe in frightening them with tales of murder and ghosts. Every human being has something of the gruesome in his composition ; the murder cases are the most popular readings in our press. I want to direct this innate desire for gruesome things to the realising of the most gruesome things in the world—the grinding of soul and body in order to gain profits, the misery of poverty and cold, the weariness of toil. If our press really wants to make its readers shudder, why does it not publish long accounts of infant mortality in the slums, of gin fed bairns, of back-doors used as fuel, of phthisical girls straining their eyes over seams ? I know why the press ignores these things, the public does not want to think of them. If the public wanted such stories every capitalist owner of a newspaper would supply them, grudgingly, but with a stern resolve to get dividends. To-day the papers are mostly run for the rich and their parasites. The only way in which 'Enery Smith can get his photograph into the papers is by jumping on Mrs. 'Enery Smith until she expires. I wonder that no criminologist has tried to prove that publicity is the greatest incentive to crime.

When I read the daily papers to my bairns I try to tell them what is left out. " Humour at Bow Street," a heading will run. Ye Gods ! Humour ! I have as much humour as most men, but if anyone can find humour in the stupid remarks of a law-giver he must be a W. W. Jacobs, a Mark Twain, a George A. Birmingham, and a Stephen Leacock rolled into one .... with the Devil thrown in. Humour at Bow Street. I have been there. I have seen the poor Magdalenes and the pitiable Lazaruses shuffle in with terror in their eyes. I have seen the inflexible mighty law condemn them to the cells, I have heard their piteous cries for mercy. And the newspapers talk of the humour of the courts.

I once read that law's primary object is to protect the rich from the poor. The appalling truth of that saying dawned on me in Bow Street. Humour ! Yes, there

is humour in Bow Street. The grimmest,
ugliest joke in the world is this.... Covent
Garden Opera House stands across the street
from the court.

*   *   *

To-day I told Senior II. to write up the
following story, I advised them to add graces
to it if they could.

"A farmer went to Edinburgh for the day.
He was walking down the High Street with
open mouth when the fire engine came swinging round the corner. The farmer gave chase
down the North Bridge and Leith Street,
and owing to the heavy traffic the engine's
rate was so slow that he could easily keep up
with it. But it turned down London Road,
and in the long silent street soon outdistanced
him. He ran until he saw that it was hopeless. Then he stopped and held up a clenched
fist.

"Ye can keep yer dawmed tattie-chips,"
he cried, "Aw'll get them some other place."

Mary Peters began thus :—

"Mr. Peter Mitchell went to Edinburgh
for the day...."

Mr. Peter Mitchell is Chairman of the School Board.

* * *

Why did I substitute " auld " for " dawmed " tattie-chips when I told the bairns the story. Art demands the " dawmed." I think I substituted the " auld " because I like a quiet life. I have no time to persuade indignant parents that " damn " is not a sin. But it was weakness on my part ; I compromised, and compromise is always a lie.

VI.

THIS morning I had a note from a farmer in the neighbourhood.

"DEAR SIR,—I send my son Andrew to get education at the school not Radical politics.

I am,

Yours respectfully,

Andrew Smith."

I called Andrew out.

"Andrew," I said, with a smile, "when you go home to-night tell your father that I hate Radicalism possibly more than he does."

The father came down to-night to apologise. "Aw thocht ye was ane o' they wheezin' Radicals," he explained. Then he added, "And what micht yer politics be ? "

"I am a Utopian," I said modestly.

He scratched his head for a moment, then he gave it up and asked my opinion of the weather. We discussed turnips for half-an-hour, at the end of which time I am sure he was wondering how an M.A. could be such an ignoramus.   We parted on friendly terms.

*   *   *

I do not think that I have any definite views on the teaching of religion to bairns; indeed, I have the vaguest notion of what religion means.   I am just enough of a Nietzschean to protest against teaching children to be meek and lowly.   I once shocked a dear old lady by saying that the part of the Bible that appealed to me most was that in which the Pharisee said: " I thank God that I am not as other men."   I was young then, I have not the courage to say it now.

I do, however, hold strongly that teaching religion is not my job.   The parish minister and the U.F. minister get good stipends for tending their flocks, and I do not see any reason in the world why I should have to look after the lambs.   For one thing I am not capable.   All I aim at is teaching bairns how to live....possibly that is the true religion; my early training prevents my getting rid of the idea that religion is intended to teach people how to die.

To-day I was talking about the probable

formation of the earth, how it was a ball of flaming gas like the sun, how it cooled gradually, how life came. A girl looked up and said: " Please, sir, what about the Bible ? " I explained that in my opinion the creation story was a story told to children, to a people who were children in understanding. I pointed out a strange feature, discovered to me by the parish minister, that the first chapter of Genesis follows the order of scientific evolution....the earth is without form, life rises from the sea, then come the birds, then the mammals.

But I am forced to give religious instruction. I confine my efforts to the four gospels ; the bairns read them aloud. I seldom make any comment on the passages.

In geography lessons I often take occasion to emphasise the fact that Muhammudans and Buddhists are not necessarily stupid folk who know no better. I cannot lead bairns to a religion, but I can prevent their being stupidly narrow.

No, I fear I have no definite opinions on religion.

I set out to enter the church, but I think that I could not have stayed in it. I fancy

that one fine Sunday morning I would have
stood up in the pulpit and said : " Friends, I
am no follower of Christ. I like fine linen
and tobacco, books and comfort. I should
be in the slums, but I am not Christlike
enough to go there. Goodbye."

I wonder ! Why then do I not stand up
and say to the School Board : " I do not
believe in this system of education at all. I
am a hypocrite when I teach subjects that I
abominate. Give me my month's screw.
Goodbye." I sigh....yet I like to fancy that
I could not have stayed in the kirk. One
thing I am sure of : a big stipend would not
have tempted me to stay. I have no wish
for money ; at least, I wouldn't go out of my
way to get it. I wouldn't edit a popular newspaper for ten thousand a year. Of that I am
sure. Quite sure. Quite.

Yet I once applied for a job on a Tory daily.
I was hungry then. What if I were hungry
now ? The flesh is weak....but, I could
always go out on tramp. I more than half
long for the temptation. Then I should
discover whether I am an idealist or a talker.
Possibly I am a little of both.

I began to write about religion, and I find

myself talking about myself. Can it be that my god is my ego ?

* * *

I began these log-notes in order to discover my philosophy of education, and I find that I am discovering myself. This discovery of self must come first. Personality goes far in teaching. May it go too far ? Is it possible that I am a danger to these bairns ? May I not be influencing them too much ? I do not think so. Anything I may say will surely be negatived at home ; my word, unfortunately, is not so weighty as father's.

In what is called Spelling Reform we cannot have a revolution; all we can hope for is a reform within Spelling, a reform that will abolish existing anomalies. So in education we cannot have a revolution. All we can hope for is a reform wrought within education by the teacher. If every teacher were a sort of Wellsian-Shavian-Nietzschean-Webbian fellow, the children would be directly under two potent influences—the parents and teachers.

" What is Truth ? " millions of Pilates have asked. It is because we have no standard of Truth that our education is a failure.   Each of us gets hold of a corner of the page of Truth, but the trouble is that so many grasp the same corner.   It is a corner dirty with thumb-marks.…" Humour in Bow Street," "Knighthood for Tooting Philanthropist," " Dastardly Act by Leeds Strikers," " Special Service of Praise in the Parish Kirk "….marks do not obliterate the page. My corner is free from thumbmarks, and anyone can read the clear type of " Christlessness in Bow Street," " Jobbery in the Sale of Honours," " Murder of Starving Strikers," " Thanksgiving Service for the Blessing of Whitechapel "….but few will read this corner's story ; the majority likes the filthy corner with the beautiful news.

I have discovered my mission.   I am the apostle of the clean corner with the dirty news written on it.

*   *   *

I began to read the second act of *An Enemy of the People* this morning, but I had to give it up ; the bairns had lost interest. I closed the book. " Suppose," I said, " suppose that this village suddenly became famous as a health-resort. People would build houses and hotels, your fathers would grow richer ; and suppose that the doctor discovered that the water supply was poisonous, that the pipes lay through a swamp where fever germs were. What would the men who had built hotels and houses say about the doctor ? What would they do about the water supply ? "

The unanimous opinion was that the water-pipes would be relaid ; the people would not want visitors to come and take fever.

This opinion leads me to conclude that bairns are idealists ; childhood takes the Christian view. Barrie says that genius is the power of being a boy again at will ; I agree, but Barrie and I are possibly thinking of different aspects. Ibsen was a genius because he became as a little child. Dr. Stockmann (Ibsen) is a simple child ; he cannot realise that self-interest can make his own brother a criminal to society.

I told my bairns what the men in the play did.

" But," said one in amazement, " they would not do that in real life ?"

" They are doing it every day," I said. " This school is old, badly ventilated, overcrowded. It is a danger to your health and mine.   Yet, if I asked for a new school, the whole village would rise up against me. ' More money on the rates ! ' they would cry, and they would treat me very much as the people in the play treated Dr. Stockmann.''

*   *   *

I find it difficult to discuss the causes of the war with the bairns.   I refuse to accept the usual tags about going to the assistance of a weak neighbour whom we agreed to protect. We all want to think that we are fighting for Belgium but are we ?

I look to Mexico and I find it has been bathed in blood because the American Oil Kings and the British Oil Kings were at war. President Diaz was pro-English, Madero was pro-American, Huerta was pro-English.... and the United States supported the notorious Villa.   Villa's rival, Carranzo, was pro-English.   It is an accepted belief that the American Oil Kings financed the first risings in order to drive the British oil interests out of the country.   Hence, widows and orphans in Mexico are the victims of a dollar massacre.

Can we trace the present war to the financiers ?   It is said that the Triple Entente is the result of Russia's receiving loans from France and Britain.

I cannot find a solution. I am inclined to attach little value to what is called national feeling. The workers are the masses, and I cannot imagine a German navvy's having any hatred of a British navvy. A world of workers would not fight, but at present the workers are so badly organised that they fight at the bidding of kings and diplomatists and financiers. War comes from the classes above, and by means of their press the upper classes convert the proletariat to their way of thinking.

A more important subject is that of the ending of wars. The idealistic vapourings of the I.L.P. with its silly talk of international-ism will do nothing to stop war. Norman Angell's cry that war doesn't pay will not stop war. But a true democracy in each country will stop it. I think of Russia with all its darkness and cruelty, and I am appalled; a true democracy there will be centuries in coming. For Germany I do not fear ; out of her militarism will surely arise a great democratic nation. And out of our own great trial a true democracy is arising. Capitalism

has failed ; the State now sees that it must
control the railways and engineering shops
in a crisis. The men who struck work on the
Clyde are of the same class as the men who
are dying in Flanders. Why should one
lot be heroes and the other lot be cursed as
traitors ? The answer is simple. The soldiers are fighting for the nation ; the engineers
are working primarily for the profiteers, and
only secondarily for the nation. Profiteering has not stood the test, and the workers
are beginning to realise the significance of its
failure.

VII.

TO-DAY I have scrapped somebody's Rural Arithmetic. It is full of sums of the How-much-will-it-take-to-paper a-room? type. This cursed utilitarianism in education riles me. Who wants to know what it will take to paper a room ? Personally I should call in the painter, and take my meals on the parlour piano for a day or two. Anyway, why this suspicion of the poor painter ? Is he worse than other tradesmen ? If we must have a utilitarian arithmetic then I want to see a book that will tell me if the watchmaker is a liar when he tells me that the mainspring of my watch is broken. I want to see sums like this :—How long will a plumber take to lay a ten foot pipe if father can do it at the rate of a yard in three minutes? (Ans., three days).

To me Arithmetic is an art not a science. I do not know a single rule ; I must always go back to first principles. I love catch questions, questions that will make a bairn think all the time. Inspectors' Tests give but little scope for the Art of Arithmetic; they are usually poor peddling things that smell strongly of materialism. In other words, they appeal to the mechanical part of a bairn's brain instead of to the imagination. I want to see a test that will include a sum like this :—$23.4 \times .065 \times 54.678 \times 0$. The cram will start in to multiply out; the imaginative bairn will glance along and see the nought, and will at once spot that the answer is zero.

*   *   *

I have just discovered an excellent song-book—Curwen's *Approved Songs*. It includes all the lovely songs of Cavalier and Puritan times, tunes like *Polly Oliver* and *Golden Slumbers*. At present my bairns are singing a Christmas Carol by Bridge, *Sweeter than Songs of Summer*. They sing treble, alto, and tenor, while I supply the bass. The time is long past Christmas, but details like that don't worry me. This carol is the sweetest piece of harmonising I have heard for a long time.

*   *   *

I have been re-reading Shaw's remarks on Sex in Education. I cannot see that he has anything very illuminating to say on the subject ; for that matter no one has. Most of us realise that something is wrong with our views on sex. The present attitude of education is to ignore sex, and the result is that sex remains a conspiracy of silence. The ideal some of us have is to raise sex to its proper position as a wondrous beautiful thing. To-day we try to convey to bairns that birth is a disgrace to humanity.

The problem before me comes to this : How can I bring my bairns to take a rational elemental view of sex instead of a conventional hypocritical one ? How can I convey to them the realisation that our virtue is mostly cowardice, that our sex morality is founded on mere respectability ? (It is the easiest thing in the world to be virtuous in Padanarum ; it is not so easy to be a saint in Oxford Street. Not because Oxford Street has more temptation, but because nobody knows you there.)

In reality I can do nothing. If I mentioned sex in school I should be dismissed at once. But if a philanthropist would come along and offer me a private school to run as I pleased, then I should introduce sex into my scheme of education. Bairns would be encouraged to believe in the stork theory of birth until they reached the age of nine. At that age they would get the naked truth.

A friend of mine, one of the cleverest men I know, and his wife, a wise woman, resolved to tell their children anything they asked. The eldest, a girl of four, asked one day where she came from. They told her, and she showed no surprise. But I would begin at nine chiefly because the stork story is so delightful that it would be cruel to deprive a bairn of it altogether. Yet, after all, the stork story is all the more charming when you know the bald truth.

Well, at the age of nine my bairns would be taken in hand by a doctor. They would learn that modesty is mainly an accidental result of the invention of clothes. They would gradually come to look upon sex as a normal fact of life ; in short, they would recognise it as a healthy thing.

Shaw is right in saying that children must get the truth from a teacher, because parents find a natural shyness in mentioning sex to

their children. But I think that the next
generation of parents will have a better
perspective ; shyness will almost disappear.
The bairns must be told ; of that there is no
doubt. The present evasion and deceit lead
to the dirtiness which constitutes the sex
education of boys and girls.

The great drawback to a frank education
on sex matters is the disgusting fact that
most grown-up people persist in associating
sex with sin. The phrase " born in sin " is
still applied to an illegitimate child. When
I think of the damnable cruelty of virtuous
married women to a girl who has had a child
I want to change the phrase into " born into
sin."

*　　*　　*

I have just discovered a section of the
Code that deals with the subject of Temperance. I smile sadly when I think that my
bairns will never have more than a pound a
week to be intemperate on. I suspect that
if I had to slave for a week for a pound I
should trek for the nearest pub on pay night ;
I should seek oblivion in some way.

Temperance ! Why waste time telling poor

bairns to be temperate? When they are fourteen they will learn that to be intemperate means the sack. If we must teach temperance let us begin at Oxford and Cambridge; at Westminster (I really forget how much wine and beer was consumed there last year; the amount raised a thirst in me at any rate).

Temperance! The profiteers see to it that the poor cannot afford to be intemperate. Coals are up now, the men who draw a royalty on each ton as it leaves the pit do not know the meaning of temperance.

I want to cry to my bairns: " Be intemperate! Demand more of the fine things of life. Don't waste time in the beershops, spend your leisure hours persuading your neighbour to help you to impose temperance on your masters."

The Code talks about food. But it does not do so honestly. I would insert the following in the Code :—

" Teachers in slum districts should point out to the children that most of their food is adulterated. Most of their boots are made of paper. Most of their clothes are made of shoddy."

*   *   *

The best thing I have found in the Code
is the section on the teaching of English. I
fancy it is the work of J. C. Smith, the Editor
of the Oxford *Spenser*. I used to have him
round at my classes; he was a first-rate
examiner. If a class had any originality
in it he drew it out. But I never forgave
J. C. Smith for editing *Much Ado About
Nothing*. He made no effort to remark on
the absurdity of the plot and motives. To
me the play is as silly as *Diplomacy* or *Our
Boys*.

"No grammar," says the Code, "should
be taught until written composition begins."
I like that, but I should re-write it thus:
"No grammar should be taught this side
the Styx."

Grammar is always changing, and the
grammar of yesterday is scrapped to-day.
A child requires to know how to speak and
how to write correctly. I can write passably
well, and when I write I do not need to know
whether a word is an adjective or an adverb,
whether a clause is a noun clause or an
adverbial clause of time modifying a certain
verb....or is it a noun? Society ladies
speak grammatically (I am told), and I'm

quite sure that not three people in the Row could tell me whether a word is a verb or an adverb (I shouldn't care to ask). The fact that I really could tell what each word is makes absolutely no difference to me. A middle-class boy of five will know that the sentence " I and nurse is going to the Pictures " is wrong.

But I must confess that grammar has influenced me in one way. I know I should say "Whom did you see?" but I always say "Who did you see?" And I used to try not to split my infinitives....until I found out that you can't split an infinitive; " to " has nothing to do with the infinitive anyway.

I want to abolish the terms Subject, Predicate, Object, Extension, Noun, Verb, &c. I fancy we could get along very well without them. Difficulties might arise in learning a foreign tongue. I don't know anything about foreign tongues; all I know is the Greek alphabet 'and a line of Homer, and the fact that all Gaul is divided into three parts. Yet I imagine that one could learn French or German as a child learns a language.

Good speaking and writing mean the correct use of idiom, and idiom is the best phrasing of the best people—best according to our standards at the present time.

I have heard Parsing and Analysis defended on the ground of their being an exercise in reasoning. I admit that they do require reasoning, but I hold that the time would be better spent in Mathematics. I hope to take my senior pupils through the first and third books of Euclid this summer. Personally, I can find much pleasure in a stiff deduction, but I find nothing but intense weariness in an analysis of sentences. My theories on education are purely personal; if *I* don't like a thing I presume that my bairns dislike it. And the strange thing is that my presumptions are nearly always right.

*   *   *

Folklore fascinates me. I find that the children of Forfarshire and Dumfriesshire have the same ring song, *The Wind and the Wind and the Wind Blows High*. I once discovered in the British Museum a book on English Folksongs, and in it I found the same song obtaining in Staffordshire. Naturally, variations occur. Did these songs all spring from a common stock? Or did incomers bring them to a district?

When I am sacked....and I half expect to be some day soon....I shall wander round the schools of Scotland collecting the folk-songs. I shall take a Punch and Judy show with me, for I know that this is a long felt want in the country. That reminds me :—a broken-down fellow came to me to-day and told pathetically how he had lost his school ...."wrongous dismissal" he called it. I wept and gave him sixpence. To-night I visited the minister. " I had a sad case in to-day," he began, " a poor fellow who had a kirk in Ross-shire. Poor chap, his wife took to drink, and he lost his kirk."

" Chap with a reddish moustache? " I asked.

" Yes, did you see him ? "

I ignored the question.

" Charity," I said, " is foolish. I don't believe in charity of that kind. You gave him something ? "

" Er—a shilling."

" You have too much heart," I said, and I took my departure.

If I have to go on tramp I shall try to live by selling sermons after school-hours.

VIII.

TO-DAY I discussed the Women's Movement with my class. They were all agreed that women should not have votes. I asked for reasons.

" They can't fight like men," said a boy.

I pointed out that they risk their lives more than men do. A woman risks her life so that life may come into the world ; a soldier risks his life so that death may come into the world.

" Women speak too much," said Margaret Steel.

" Read the Parliamentary debates," said I.

" Women have not the brains," said a boy.

I made no reply, I lifted his last exam. paper, and showed the class his 21 per cent, then I showed him Violet Brown's 93 per cent. But I was careful to add that the illustration was not conclusive.

I went on to tell them that the vote was

of little use to men, and that I did not consider it worth striving for. But I tried to
show them that the Women's Movement was
a much bigger thing than a fight for political
power. It was a protest against the system
that made sons doctors and ministers, and
daughters typists and shopgirls, that made
girls black their idle brothers' boots, that
offered £60 to a lady teacher who was doing
as good work as the man in the next room
with his £130. I did not take them to the
deeper topics of Marriage, Inheritance, the
economic dependence of women on men that
makes so many marry for a home. But I
tried to show that owing to woman's being
voteless the laws are on the man's side, and
I instanced the Corporation Baths in the
neighbouring city. There only one day a
week is set aside for women. Then it struck
me that perhaps the women of the city have
municipal votes, and I suggested that if this
were the case, women are less interested in
cold water than men, a circumstance that
goes to show that women have a greater
need of freedom than I thought they
had.

On the whole it was a disappointing dis-
cussion.

       *   *   *

I went up to see Lawson of Rinsley School
to-night. I talked away gaily about having
scrapped my Readers and Rural Arithmetic.
He was amused; I know that he considers
me a cheerful idiot. But he grew serious when
I talked about my Socialism.

" You blooming Socialists," he said, with
a dry laugh, " are the most cocky people I
have yet struck. You think you are the
salt of the earth and that all the others are
fatheads."

" Quite right, Lawson," I said with a
laugh. And I added seriously : " You see,
my boy, that if you have a theory, you've
simply *got* to think the other fellow an idiot.
I believe in Socialism—the Guild Socialism
of *The New Age*, and naturally I think that
Lloyd George and Bonar Law and the Cecils,
and all that lot are hopelessly wrong."

" Do you mean to tell me that you are a
greater thinker than Arthur James Balfour ? "
Lawson sat back in his chair and watched
the effect of this shot.

I considered for a minute.

" It's like this," I said slowly, " you really cannot compare a duck with a rabbit.   You can't say that Shakespeare is greater than Napoleon or Burns than Titian.   Balfour is a good man in his own line, and—"

" And you ? "

" I sometimes think of great things," I replied modestly.   " Balfour has an ideal ; he believes, as Lord Roberts believed, in the Public Schools, in Oxford and Cambridge, in the type of Englishman who becomes an Imperialist Cromer.   He believes in the aristocracy, in land, in heredity of succession. His ideal, so far as I can make out, is to have an aristocracy that behaves kindly and charitably to a deserving working - class— which, after all, is Nietzsche's ideal.

I believe in few of these things.   I detest charity of that kind ; I hate the type of youth that our Public Schools and Oxfords turn out.   I want to see the land belong to the people, I want to see every unit of the State working for the delight that work, as opposed to toil, can bring.   The aristocracy has merits that I appreciate.   Along with the poor they cheerfully die for their country.... it is the profiteering class with

its "Business as Usual" cant that I want
to slay. I want to see all the excellent
material that exists in our aristocracy turned
to nobler uses than bossing niggers in India
so that millionaires at home may be multi-
millionaires, than wasting time and wealth
in the social rounds of London."

"Are you a greater thinker than Balfour?"
I sighed

"I think I have a greater ideal," I said.
"And," I added, "I am sure that if Balfour
were asked about it he would reply: 'I
wish I could have got out of my aristocratic
environment at your age.'"

"Lawson," I continued, "I gathered tatties
behind the digger once. That is the chief
difference between me and Balfour. When
first I went through Eton on a motor-bus
and saw the boys on the playing grounds, I
said to myself, 'Thank God I wasn't sent to
Eton!'"

"Class prejudice and jealousy," said Lawson. "Will the Rangers get into the Final?"

* * *

I met Wilkie the mason, on the road
to-night. He cannot write his name, and
he is the richest man in the village.

"What's this Aw hear aboot you bein'
ane o' they Socialists?" he demanded.
"Aw didna ken that when Aw voted for
ye."

"If you had?"

"Not a vote wud ye hae gotten frae me.
Ye'll be layin' yer bombs a' ower the place,"
he said half jocularly.

"Ye manna put ony o' they ideas in the
bairns' heids," he continued anxiously. "Politics have no place in a schule."

I did not pursue the subject; I side-
tracked him on to turnips, and by using what
I had picked up from Andrew Smith I made
a fairly good effort. When we parted Wilkie
grasped my hand.

"Ye're no dozzent," he said kindly, "but,
tak ma advice, and leave they politics alone.
It's a dangerous game for a schulemester to
play."

* * *

I find that I am becoming obsessed by
my creed. I see that I place politics before
everything else in education. But I feel
that I am doing the best I can for true education After all it isn't Socialism I am teach-

ing, it is heresy. I am trying to form minds
that will question and destroy and rebuild.

Morris's *News from Nowhere* appeals to me
most as a Utopia. Like him I want to see
an artistic world.

I travelled to Newcastle on Saturday, and
the brick squalor that stretches for miles
out Elswick and Blaydon way sickened me.
Dirty bairns were playing on muddy patches,
dirty women were gossiping at doors, miners
were wandering off in twos and threes with
whippets at their heels. And smoke was
over all. Britain is the workshop of the
world. Good old Merrie England !

These are strange entries for a Dominie's
Log. I must bring my mind back to Vulgar
Fractions and Composition.

*   *   *

There was a Cinema Show in the village
hall to-night. My bairns turned out in force.
Most of the pictures were drivel ....the typist
wrongly accused, the seducing employer ; the
weeping parents at home. The average cinema
plot is of the same brand as the plots in a
washerwoman's weekly. Then we had the
inevitable Indian chase on horseback, and

the hero pardoned after the rope was round his neck.

I enjoyed the comic films. To see the comic go down in diver's dress to wreck a German submarine was delightfully ludicrous. He took off his helmet under water and wiped the sweat from his brow. Excellent fun !

I have often thought about the cinema as an aid to education. At the present time it is a drag on education, for its chief attraction is its piffling melodrama. Yet I have seen good plays and playlets filmed....that is good melodramatic and incident plays.

I have seen *Hamlet* filmed, and then I understood what Tolstoi (or was it Shaw ?) meant when he said that Shakespeare without his word music is nowhere. Yet I must be just ; philosophy had to go along with music when the cinema took up *Hamlet*.

The cinema may have a future as an educational force, but it will deal with what I consider the subsidiary part of education— the facts of life. Pictures of foreign countries are undoubtedly of great use. The cinema can never give us theories and philosophy. So with its lighter side. *Charley's Aunt* might make a good film ; *The Importance of Being Earnest* could not. The cinema can give us humour but not wit. What will happen when the cinema and the phonograph are made to work together perfectly I do not know. I may yet be able to take my bairns to a performance of *Nan* or *The Wild Duck* or *The Doctor's Dilemma*.

* * *

" Please, sir, Willie Smith was swearing." Thus little Maggie Shepherd to me to-day.

I always fear this complaint, for what can I do ? I can't very well ask Maggie what he said, and if he says he wasn't swearing.. well, his word is as good as Maggie's. I can summon witnesses, but bairns have but the haziest notion of what swearing is. (For that matter so do I.) If a boy shoves his fingers to his nose...." Please, sir, he swore ! "

I try to be a just man, and....well, I was bunkered at the ninth hole on Saturday, and I dismissed Willie Smith—without an admonition. But I am worried to-night, for I can't recollect whether Willie has ever caddied for me ; I have a shrewd suspicion that he has.

IX.

THE word " republican " came up to-day in a lesson, and I asked what it meant. Four girls told me that their fathers were republicans, but they had no idea of the meaning of the word. One lassie thought that it meant " a man who is always quarrelling with the Tories "....a fairly penetrating definition.

I explained the meaning of the word, and said that a republican in this country was wasting his time and energy. I pointed to America with its Oil Kings, Steel Kings, Meat Kings, and called it a country worse than Russia. I told of the corruption of politics in France.

Then I rambled on to Kings and Kingship. It is a difficult subject to tackle even with children, but I tried to walk warily. I said that the notion of a king was for people in an elementary stage of development. Intellectual folk have no use for all the pomp and pageantry of kingship. Royalty as it exists to-day is bad for us and for the royal family. The poor princes and princesses are reared in an atmosphere of make-believe. Their individuality and their loves are crushed by a system. And it is really a system of lies. " In the King's name ! " Why make all this pretence when everyone knows that it is " In the Cabinet's name " ? It is not fair to the king.

I am no republican ; I do not want to see monarchy abolished in this land. I recognise that monarchy is necessary to the masses. But I want to bring my bairns to see monarchy stripped of its robes, its pageantry, its remoteness, its circumstance. Loyalty is a name to most of us. People sing the National Anthem in very much the same way as they say Grace before Meat. The Grace-sayer is thinking of his dinner ; the singer is wondering if he'll manage to get out in time to collar a taxi.

I do not blame the kings ; I blame their advisers. We are kept in the dark by them. We hear of a monarch's good deeds, but we never hear the truth about him. The unwritten law demands that the truth shall be

kept secret until a few generations have
passed. I know nothing about the king. I
don't know what he thinks of Republicanism
(in his shoes I should be a red-hot Republican),
Socialism, Religion, Morals; and I want to
know whether he likes Locke's novels or
Galsworthy's drama. In short, I want to
know the man that must of necessity be
greater than the king. I am tired of pro-
cessions and functions.

I became a loyalist when first I went to
Windsor Castle. Three massed bands were
playing in the quadrangle; thousands of
visitors wandered around. The King came to
the window and bowed. I wanted to go up
and take him by the arm and say : " Poor
King, you are not allowed to enjoy the sensa-
tion of being in a crowd, you are an abstrac-
tion, you are behind a barrier of nobility
through which no commoner can pass. Come
down and have a smoke with me amongst all
these typists and clerks." And I expect
that every man and woman in that crowd
was thinking : " How nice it must be to be
a king ! "

Yet if a king were to come down from the
pedestal on which the courtiers have placed

him, I fear that the people would scorn him. They would cry : " He is only a man ! " I am forced to the conclusion that pomp and circumstance are necessary after all. The people are to blame. The King is all right ; he looks a decent, kindly soul with a good heart. But the people are not interested in good hearts ; the fools want gilt coaches and crimson carpets and all the rubbish of show.

*　　*　　*

A lady asked me to-day whether I taught my children manners. I told her that I did not. She asked why. I replied that manners were sham, and my chief duty was to get rid of sham. Then she asked me why I lifted my hat to her....and naturally I collapsed incontinently. Once again I write the words, " It is a difficult thing to be a theorist....and an honest man at the same time."

On reflection I think that it is a case of personality *versus* the whole community. No man can be consistent. Were I to carry my convictions to their natural con- clusion I should be an outcast....and an outcast is of no value to the community. I lift my hat to a lady not because I respect her

(I occasionally do.   I always doff my hat to
the school charwoman, but I am rather
afraid of her), but because it is not worth
while to protest against the little things of
life.   Incidentally, the whole case against
hat-lifting is this :—In the lower and lower
middle classes the son does not lift his hat
to his mother though he does to the minister's
wife.

No, I do not teach manners.   If a boy
" Sirs " me, he does it of his own free will.
I believe that you cannot teach manners ;
taught manners are always forced, always
overdone.   My model of a true gentleman is
a man with an innate good taste and artistry.
My idea of a lady....well, one of the truest
ladies I have yet known kept a dairy in the
Canongate of Edinburgh.

I try to get my bairns to do to others as
they would like others to do to them. Shaw
says " No : their tastes may not be the same
as yours."   Good old G. B. S. !

I once was in a school where manners were
taught religiously.   I whacked a boy one
day.   He said, " Thank you, sir."

*   *   *

I wonder how much influence on observation the so-called Nature Study has.   At one time I attended a Saturday class.   We went botanising.   I learned nothing about Botany, but that was because Margaret was there.   I observed much....her eyes were grey and her eyelashes long.   We generally managed to lose the class in less than no time.   Yet we did pretend.   She was pretending to show me the something or other marks on a horse-chestnut twig when I first kissed her.   She is married now.   I don't believe in Saturday excursions.

I got up my scanty Nature Study from Grant Allen's little shilling book on plants. It was a delightful book full of an almost Yankee imagination.   It theorised all the way....grass developed a long narrow blade so that it might edge its way to the sun ; wild tobacco has a broad blade because it doesn't need to care tuppence for the competition of other plants, it can grow on wet clay of railway bankings.   I think now that Grant Allen was a romancer not a scientist.

I do not see the point in asking bairns to count the stamens of a buttercup (Dr. Johnson hated the poets who " count the streaks of the tulip ").   But I do want to

make them Grant Allens; I want them to
make a theory.   Nature Study has but little
result unless bairns get a lead.   No boy will
guess that the lines on a petal are intended
to lead bees to the honey; at least, I know
I would never have guessed it.   I should
never have guessed that flowers are beautiful
or perfumed in order to attract insects.   But
I am really no criterion.   I could not tell at
this moment the colour of my bedroom wall-
paper; I can't tell whether my father wears
a moustache or side-whiskers.   Until I began
to teach Woodwork I never observed a
mortise, or if I did, I never wondered how it
was made.   I never noticed that the tops
of houses sloped downward until I took up
Perspective.

Anyway, observation is a poor attainment
unless it is combined with genius as in
Darwin's case.   Sherlock Holmes is a nobody.
Observation should follow fancy.   The average youth has successive hobbies.   He takes
up photography, and is led (sometimes) to
enquire into the action of silver salts; he
takes up wood-carving, and begins to find
untold discoveries in the easy-chair.

I would advocate the keeping of animals

at school. 1 would have a rabbit run, a pigeon loft, one or two dogs, and a few cats for the girls. Let a boy keep homers and fly them, and he will observe much. Apart from the observation side of the question I would advocate a live stock school-farm on humanitarian grounds ; every child would acquire a sense of duty to animals. I am sure all my bairns would turn out on a Sunday to feed their pets. And what a delightful reward for kindness....make a boy or girl " Feeder-in-Chief " for the week ! Incident-ally, the study of pigeons and rabbits would conduce to a frank realisation of sex.

* * *

1 have just bought the new shilling edition of H. G. Wells's *New Worlds for Old*, and I have come upon this passage...." ....Socia-lists turn to the most creative profession of all, to that great calling which, with each generation, renews the world's 'circle of ideas,' the Teachers ! "

But why he puts the mark of exclamation at the end I do not know.

On the same page he says : " The construc-tive Socialist logically declares the teacher master of the situation."

If the Teachers are masters of the situation
I wish every teacher in Scotland would get
The New Age each week.   Orage's *Notes of
the Week* are easily the best commentary on
the war I have seen.   *The New Age* is so
very amusing, too ;   its band of " warm young
men " are the kind who " can't stand Nietzsche
because of his damnable philanthropy " as
a journalist friend of mine once phrased it.
They despise Shaw and Wells and Webb....
the old back-numbers.   The magazine is
pulsating with life and youth.   Every con-
tributor is so cock-sure of himself.   It is the
only fearless journal I know ;   it has no
advertisements, and with advertisements a
journal is muzzled.

*   *   *

One or two bairns are going to try the
bursary competition of the neighbouring
Secondary School, and I have just got hold
of the last year's papers.

" Name an important event in British
History for each of any eight of the following
years :—1314, 1688, 1759, &c.".... and Wells
says that teaching is the most creative
profession of all !

" Write an essay of twenty lines or so on

any one of these subjects :—School, Holidays, Examinations, Bursaries, Books." The examiners might have added a few other bright interesting topics such as Truth, Morals, Faith, Courage.

" Name the poem to which each of the following lines belongs, and add, if you can, the next line in each case, &c." There are ten lines, and I can only spot six of them. And I am, theoretically, an English scholar ; I took an Honours English Degree under Saintsbury. But my degree is only a second class one ; that no doubt accounts for my lack of knowledge.

That the compilers of the paper are not fools is shown by the fact that they ask a question like this :—" A man loses a dog, you find it ; write and tell him that you have found it."

The Arithmetic paper is quite good. My bairns are to fail ; I simply cannot teach them to answer papers like these.

X.

I TRIED an experiment to-day. I gave an exam. in History, and each pupil was allowed to use a text-book. The best one was first, she knew what to select. I deprecate the usual exam. system of allotting a prescribed time to each paper. Blyth Webster, the racy young lecturer in English in Edinburgh University, used to allow us an indefinite time for our Old English papers. I generally required a half hour to give him all I knew about Old English, but I believe that some students sat for five hours. Students write and think at different rates, and the time limit is always unjust.

I wish the Department would allow me to set the Higher Grade Leavings English papers for once. My paper would certainly include the following :—

" If Shakespeare came back to earth what do you think would be his opinion of Women's Suffrage (refer to *The Taming of the Shrew*) Home Rule, Sweated Labour, the Kaiser ? "

" Have you read any Utopia ?   If not, it doesn't matter ;   write one of your own. (Note....a Utopia is an ideal country—this side the grave.)

" Discuss Spenser's idea of chivalry, and state what you think would be his opinion on table manners, Soho, or any slum you know, " the Present State of Ireland."

" What would Burns have thought of the prevalence of the kilt among the Semitic inhabitants of Scotland ?   Is Burns greater than Harry Lauder ?   Tell me why you think he isn't or is."

" Discuss the following humorists and alleged humorists :—Dickens, Jacobs, Lauder, Jerome, Leacock, Storer Clouston, Wells (in *Kipps*, and *Mr. Polly*), Locke (in *Septimus*), Bennett (in *The Card*), Mark Twain, your class teacher, the average magistrate."

" If you have not read any humour at all, write a humorous dialogue between a brick and the mongrel dog it came in contact with."

I hold that my exam. paper would discover any genius knocking about in ignorance of his or her powers. I intend to offer it to the Department....when I am out of the profession.

* * *

It is extremely difficult for any teacher to keep from getting into a rut. The continual effort to make things simple and elementary for children is apt to deaden the intellect.

To-night I felt dull; I simply couldn't think. So I took up a volume of Nietzsche, and I now know the remedy for dullness. Nietzsche is a genius; he dazzles one....and he almost persuades. To-night I am doubting. Is my belief in a great democracy all wrong? Is it true that there is a slave class that can never be anything else? Is our Christian morality a slave morality which is evolving the wrong type of human?

I think of the pity and kindness which is making us keep alive the lunatic and the incurable; I am persuaded to believe that our hospitals are in the long run conducing to an unfit race. Unfit physically; but unfit mentally? Is Sandow the Superman? Will Nietzsche's type of Master man with his physical energy and warlikeness prove to be the best?

I think that the journalists who are anathe-
matising Nietzsche are wrong; I don't believe
the Kaiser ever read a line of his. But I
think that every German is subconsciously
a believer in energy and " Master Morality " ;
Nietzsche was merely one who realised his
nature. The German religion is undoubtedly
the religion of the Old Testament ; to them
" good " is all that pertains to power ; their
God is the tyrant of the Old Testament.
Nietzsche holds that the New Testament code
of morals was invented by a conquered race ;
the poor were meek and servile, and they
looked forward to a time when they would be
in glory while the rich man frizzled down
below.

No man can scorn Nietzsche ; you are
forced to listen to him. Only fools can
dismiss him with the epithet " Madman ! "

But I cannot follow him ; I believe that if
pity and kindness are wrong, then wrong is
right. Yet I see that Nietzsche is wise in
saying that there must always be one stone
at the top of the pyramid. The question is
this :—Will a democracy always be sure to
choose the right man ? I wonder.

I found one arresting statement in the

book :—" If we have a degenerate mean environment, the fittest will be the man who is best adapted to degeneracy and meanness ; he will survive." That is what is happening now. I believe that the people will one day be capable of altering this basis of society ; Nietzsche believed that the people are mostly of the slave variety, and that a better state of affairs could only come about through the breeding of Supermen....masters. " The best shall rule," says he. Who are the best ? I ask, and I really cannot answer myself.

* * *

As I go forward with these notes I find that I become more and more impelled to write down thoughts that can only have a remote connection with the education of children. I think the explanation lies in the fact that every day I realise more and more the futility of my school-work. Indeed, I find myself losing interest sometimes ; I go through a lesson on Geography mechanically ; in short, I drudge occasionally. But I always awake at Composition time.

I find it useless to do home correction ; a bairn won't read the blue pencil marks. I must sit down beside him while I correct ;

and this takes too much time....from a time-table point of view.

But the mistakes in spelling and grammar are minor matters, what I look for are ideas. I never set a dull subject of the How-I-spent-my-holidays type ; every essay must appeal to the imagination. " Suppose you go to sleep for a thousand years," I said, " and tell the story of your awaking." I asked my Qualifying to become invisible ; most of them took to thieving and spying. I gave them Wells's *The Invisible Man* and *When the Sleeper Wakes* to read later.

" Go to Mrs. Rabbit's Garden Party, and describe it." One boy went as a wolf, and returned with the party inside. A girl went as a weasel and left early because she could not eat the lettuce and cabbage on the table. One boy went as an elephant and could not get in.

" Write a child of seven's account of wash-ing day," I said to my Qualifying, and I got some delightful baby-talk from Margaret Steel and Violet Brown.

" Imagine that you are the last man left alive on earth." This essay produced some good work ; most of the girls were concerned about the fact that there was no one to bury them when they died.

The best results of all came from this subject:—"Die at the age of ninety, and write the paragraph about yourself to the local paper." Most of them made the present minister make a few pious remarks from the pulpit ; one girl was clever enough to name a strange minister.

A newspaper correspondence interests a class. "Make a Mr. James Smith write a letter to *The Scotsman* saying that he saw a cow smoking a cigar one night ; then write the replies." One boy made a William Thomson suggest that a man must have been standing beside the cow in the darkness. Smith replied that this was impossible, for any man standing beside a cow would be a farmer or a cattleman, and "neither of them can afford to smoke cigars."

*   *   *

I notice that many School Boards insist on having Trained Teachers. Is it possible to "train" a teacher ? Are teachers not born like poets ? I think they are. I have seen untrained teachers at work, and I have seen trained teachers ; I never observed a scrap of difference. All I would say to a young teacher is : " Ask questions. Ask why there is a fence round the field, ask why there is a fence round that tree in the field, then ask whether any plant or tree has a natural fence of its own."

And I think I should say this : " A good teacher will begin a lesson on Cromwell, touch, in passing, Jack Johnson, Charlie Chaplin, Votes for Women, guinea pigs, ghosts, and finish up with an enquiry into Protective Coloration of Animals."

The Code seems to be founded on the assumption that the teachers of Scotland don't know their business. Why specify that Nature Study will be taught ? Any good teacher will refer to Nature every five minutes of the day. To me teaching is a ramble through every subject the teacher knows.

No, I don't think a teacher can be trained, but I am prejudiced ; I took the Acting Teachers' Certificate Exam....and passed Third Class. In the King's Scholarship I was ninety-ninth in the list of a hundred and one. Luckily, the Acting Teachers' list was given in alphabetical order.

I had a friend at the university, Anderson

was his name, a medical. He had passed in Physics, and naturally his name was near the beginning of the list. His local paper had it " A Brilliant Student." Anderson got through at the ninth shot.

* * *

To-day I talked about crime and punishment. I told my bairns that a criminal cannot help himself ; heredity and environment make a man good or bad. I spoke of the environment that makes millions of children diseased morally and physically, and of the law that punishes a man for the sins of the community. I told them that there should be no prisons ; if a man is a murderer he is not responsible for his actions, and he must be confined....but not in prison.

Our present system is not justice ; it is vengeance. I once saw a poor waif sent to prison for stealing a pair of boots, sent to the care of warders, sent to acquire a hatred of his fellowmen. Justice would have asked : " Why did he steal ? Why had he no boots ? What sort of life has he been forced to lead ? " and I know that the waif would have been acquitted.

I told my bairns that to cure any evil you must get at the root of it, and I incidentally pointed to the Insurance Act, and said that it was like treating a man with a suppurating appendix for the headache that was one of the symptoms.   I told them that their fathers have not tried to get at the root of evil, that their prisons and cats and oakum are cowardly expedients.   The evil is that the great majority of people are poor slaves, while the minority live on their earnings.   That isn't politics ; it is truth.   I told them that if I had been born in the Cowgate of Edinburgh I should have been a thief and a drunkard.... and society would have added to my curse of heredity and environment the pains and brutishness of a prison.   And yet men accuse me of attaching too much importance to material reforms.

*   *   *

I have not used the strap for many weeks now.   I hope that I shall never use it again. I found a boy smoking a cigarette to-day. Four years ago I should have run him into the school and welted him.   To-day I spoke to him.   " Joseph," I said, " I smoke myself, and at your age I smoked an occasional Wood-

bine.   But it isn't really good for a boy, and
I hope you won't get into the habit of buying
cigs. with your pocket money." He smiled
and told me that he didn't really like it ; he
just smoked for fun.   And he tossed the cigarette over a wall.

A very clever friend of mine talks about
the " Hamlet cramp." I've got it. Other
men have a definite standard of right and
wrong ; I have none.   The only original sin
that I believe in is the cruelty that has come
to man from the remote tree-dweller.

XI.

A VILLAGER stopped me on my way to school this morning. " Look at that," he cried, pointing to a broken branch on a tree in his garden, " that's what comes o' yer nae discipline ideas. That's ane o' yer laddies that put his kite into ma gairden. Dawm it, A'll no stand that ! Ye'll jest go doon to the school and gie that boy the biggest leathering that he's ever had in his life."

I explained patiently that I was not the village constable, and I told him that the broken branch had nothing to do with me. He became angry, but he became speechless when I said, " I sympathise with you. Had it been my garden I should have sworn possibly harder than you have done. On the other hand, had it been twenty years ago and my kite, well, I should have done exactly what the boy did. Good morning."

Although it was no concern of mine I called the boy out, and advised him to try to think of other people. Then I addressed the bairns. " You might convey to your parents," I said, " that I am not the policeman in this village ; I'm a schoolmaster."

I think that many parents are annoyed at my giving up punishment. They feel that I am not doing their work for them ; they think that the dominie should do the training of children....other people's children, not their own. I find that I am trying to do a very difficult thing. The home influence is bad in many cases ; the children hear their parents slight the teacher, and they do not know what to think. The average parent looks upon the teacher as an enemy. If I hit a boy the parents side with him, if I don't hit the boy who hit their boy, they indignantly ask what education is coming to. Many a night I feel disheartened. I find that I am on the side of the bairns. I am against law and discipline ; I am all for freedom of action.

* * *

At last I have attained my ambition. As a boy my great ambition was to possess a cavalry trumpet and bugle. I have just

bought both. I call the bairns to school
with " Stables " or the " Fall In," and I glee-
fully look forward to playtime so that I may
have another tootle. The bairns love to
hear the calls, but I think I enjoy them most.

I try hard to share the bairns' joys. At
present I am out with them every day
flying kites, and I never tire of this. The
boys bring me their comic papers, but I find
that I cannot laugh at them as I used to do.
Yet, I like to see *Chips;* Weary Willie and
Tired Tim are still figuring on the front
page, but their pristine glory is gone. When
I first knew them they were the creation of
Tom Browne, and no artist can follow Tom
in his own line.

I miss the old " bloods " ; I used to glory
in the exploits of Frank Reade and Deadwood
Dick. I have sat on a Sunday with *Deadwood
Dick* in the covers of a family Bible, and my
old grandmother patted my head and told
me I was a promising lad.

Then there was Buffalo Bill—tuppence
coloured ; I never see his name now. I
wonder why so many parents and teachers
cuff boys' heads when they find them reading
comic papers and " bloods." I see no harm

in either.   I wish that people would get out
of the absurd habit of taking it for granted
that whatever a boy does is wrong.   I hold
that a boy is nearly always right.

I see in to-day's *Scotsman* that a Sheriff
substitute in Edinburgh has sentenced two
brothers of nine and ten to twelve stripes with
the birch rod for stealing tuppence ha'penny.
The account remarked that the brothers had
previously had a few stripes for a similar
theft.   That punishment is no prevention is
proved in this case.

The Sheriff Substitute must have a very
definite idea of righteousness ; I envy him his
conscience free from all remembrance of
shortcomings in the past.   For my part had I
been sitting in judgment on the poor laddies
I should have recollected the various times
I have travelled first with a third ticket,
sneaked into circuses by lifting the tent cover,
laid farthings on the railway so that they
might become ha'pennies, or, with a special
piece of luck—a goods train—pennies.   Then
I should have invited the boys to tea, and
sent them home with *Comic Cuts*, two oranges,
and a considerable bit of chewing gum.
Anyhow, my method would have brought out

any good in the boys. The method of the judge will bring out no good ; it may make the boys feel that they are enemies of society. And I should like to ask the gentleman what he would do if his young son stole the jam. I'm sure he would not send for the birch rod. The damnable thing about the whole affair is that he is probably a very nice kindly man who would not whip a dog with his own hand. His misfortune is his being part of a system.

* * *

I have just added a few volumes to my school library. I tried to recollect the books that I liked as a youth ; then I wrote for catalogues of " sevenpennies." The new books include these :—*The Prisoner of Zenda* and its sequel, *Rupert of Hentzau*, *King Solomon's Mines*, *Montezuma's Daughter*, *The Four Feathers*, *A Gentleman of France*, *White Fang*, *The Call of the Wild*, *The Invisible Man*, *The War of the Worlds*, *The War in the Air*, *Dr. Nikola*, *A Bid for Fortune*, *Micah Clarke*. I find that the average bairn of thirteen cannot appreciate these stories. Margaret Steel was the only one who read *The Scarlet Pimpernel* and asked for the sequel. Most of them stuck half way with *Zenda*. Guy Boothby's novels, the worst of the lot possibly, appealed to them strongly. The love element bores the boys, but the girls rather like it. One boy sat and yawned over *King Solomon's Mines ;* then he took out a coloured comic and turned to the serial. I took the book away and told him to read the serial. Violet Brown prefers a book about giants from the infant room to all the romantic stories extant. After all, they are but children.

* * *

I am delighted with my sketching results. We go out every Wednesday and Friday afternoon, and many bairns are giving me good work. We usually end up with races or wading in the sea. There was much wonder when first they saw my bare feet, but now they take my feet for granted.

Modesty is strong here. The other day the big girls came to me and asked if they could come to school slipshod.

" You can come in your nighties for all I care," I said, and they gasped.

We sit outside all day now. My classes take books and wander away down the road and lie on the banks. When I want them I call with the bugle. Each class has a " regimental call," and they come promptly. They most of them sit down separately, but the chatterers like to sit together.

I force no bairn to learn in my school. The few who dislike books and lessons sit up when I talk to the class. The slackers are not always the most ignorant.

I am beginning to compliment myself on having a good temper. For the past six weeks I have left the manual room open at playtime and the boys have made many toys. But they have made a woeful mess of the cutting tools. It is trying to find that your favourite plane has been cracked by a boy who has extreme theories on the fixing of plane irons. But it is very comforting to know that the School Board will have to pay for the damage. Yes, my temper is excellent.

*   *   *

On Saturday I went to a Bazaar, and various members of the aristocracy talked to me. They talked very much in the manner they talk to their gardeners, and I was led to muse upon the social status of a dominie. What struck me most was the fact that they imitate royalty in the broaching of topics of conversation ; I knew that I presumed

when I entered new ground of conversation.
The ladies were very polite and very regal,
and very well pleased with themselves. One
of them said : " I hope that you do your best
to make these children realise that there are
classes in society ; so many of their parents
refuse to see the good in other classes ! "

" For my part," I answered, " I acknow-
ledge one aristocracy—the aristocracy of
intellect. I teach my children to have respect
for thinking." She stared at me, and went
away.

I am not prejudiced against the county
people, but any superiority of manner annoys
me. I simply have no use for ladies who live
drifting lives. The lady-bountifuls, or should
it be the ladies-bountiful ? of Britain would
be much better as typists ; in these days of
alleged scarcity of labour they might come
down and mix with the lower orders. Their
grace and breeding would do much to improve
us, and we might be able to help them in
some ways. I am not being cynical, I have
a genuine admiration for the breeding and
beauty of some society women.

The doctor and the minister are seldom
patronised. I cannot for the life of me see

why it is more lowly to cure a child of ignorance than measles.

I have heard it said that the real reason of the teacher's low social status is the fact that very often he is the son of a humble labourer. There is some truth in this. At the Training College and the University the student meets men of his own class only; he never learns the little tricks of deportment that make up society's criterion of a gentleman. But for my part I blame the circumstances under which a dominie works. In Scotland he is the servant of a School Board, and a School Board is generally composed of men who have but the haziest notion of the meaning of education. That is bad enough, but very often there is a feud between one or two members and the teacher. Perhaps the teacher does not get his coals from Mr. Brown the Chairman, perhaps Mr. Brown voted for another man when the appointment was made. It is difficult for a man who is ruled by a few low-idealed semi-illiterate farmers and pig-dealers to emphasise his social position.

Larger areas have been spoken of by politicians. Personally, I don't want larger areas;

I want to see the profession run by the members, just as Law and Medicine are. It is significant that the medical profession has dropped considerably in the social scale since it allowed itself to work under the Insurance Act.

My ideal is an Education Guild which will replace the Scotch Education Department. It will draw up its own scheme of instruction, fix the salaries of its members, appoint its own inspectors, build its own schools. It will be directly responsible to the State which will remain the supreme authority.

I blame the teachers for their low social status. To-day they have no idea of corporate action. They pay their subscriptions to their Institute, and for the most part talk of stopping them on the ground that it is money wasted. The authorities of the Institute try to work for a better union, but they try clumsily and stodgily. They never write or talk forcibly ; they resemble the Labour Members of Parliament in their having an eager desire to be respectable at any price. I don't know why it is, but when a professional man tries to put his thoughts on paper he almost always succeeds in saying nothing in many fine phrases.

What is really wrong with the Educational Institute of Scotland is hoary-headedness. It is run by old men and old wives. A big man in the Institute is usually a teacher with thirty years' experience as a headmaster. Well....if a man can teach under the present system for thirty years and retain any originality or imagination at the end of that time he must be a genius.

I object to age and experience; I am all for youth and empiricism. After all, what is the use of experience in teaching? I could bet my boots that ninety-nine out of a hundred teachers use the methods they learned as pupil-teachers. Experience! I have heard dominies expatiate on innovations like Kindergarten and Blackboard Drawing. I still have to meet a dominie of experience who has any name but " fad " for anything in education later than 1880.

I have never tried to define the word " fad." I should put it thus :—A fad is a half-formed idea that a sub-inspector has borrowed from a bad translation of a distinguished foreigner's treatise on Education, and handed on to a deferential dominie.

*　　*　　*

An inspector called to-day; a middle-aged kindly gentleman with a sharp eye. His chief interest in life was tables.

"How many pence in fifty-seven farthings?" he fired at my highest class. When he found that they had to divide mentally by four, he became annoyed.

"They ought to know their tables," he said to me.

"What tables?" I asked.

"O, they should learn up that; why I can tell you at once what sixty-nine farthings are."

I explained humbly that I couldn't, and should never acquire the skill.

I did not like his manner of talking *at* the teacher through the class. When an inspector says, "You ought to know this," the scholars glance at the teacher, for they are shrewd enough to see that the teacher is being condemned.

He fired his parting shot as he went out.

"You must learn not to talk in school," he said.

I am a peaceful man, and I hate a scene. I said nothing, but I shall do nothing. If he returns he will find no difference in the school.

The bairns did talk to each other when the inspector talked to me, but when he asked for attention he got it.

I am surprised to find that his visit does not worry me ; I have at last lost my fear of the terror of teaching—H.M.I.S.

XII.

I WENT "drumming" last night. I like the American word "drummer," it is so much more expressive than our "commercial traveller."

I made a series of postcards, and I went round the shops trying to place them. One man refused to take them up because the profits would not be large enough. As the profits work out at 41½ per cent I begin to wonder what he usually makes.

To-day I talked to the bairns about commerce, and I· pointed out that much in commerce was thieving.

"This is commerce," I said : "Suppose I am a pig-dealer. I hear one day from a friend that pigs will rise in price in a few days. I at once set out on a tour of neighbouring farms, and by nightfall I have bought twenty pigs at the market price. Next morning pigs have doubled in price, and these farmers naturally want to shoot me. Why don't they shoot me ? "

" They would be hanged," said Violet Brown.

" Because they would buy pigs in the same way if they had the chance," said Margaret Steel.

I went on to say that buying pigs like that is stealing, and I said that the successful business man is usually the man who is most unscrupulous.

I told them of the murderous system that allows a big firm to place a shop next door to a small merchant and undersell him till his business dies. It is all done under the name of competition, but of course there is no more competition about the affair than there is about the relationship between a wolf and a lamb.

I try very very hard to keep my bairns from low ideals. Some one, Oscar Wilde or Shaw, I think, says that love of money is the root of all good. That is the sort of paradox that isn't true, and not even funny. I see farmers growing rich on child labour : fifteen pence a day for spreading manure. I meet the poor little boys of thirteen and fourteen on the road, and the smile has gone from their faces; their bodies are bent and racked.

When I was thirteen I went to the potato-gathering at a farm. Even now, when I pass a field where potatoes are being lifted, the peculiar smell of potato earth brings back to me those ten days of misery. I seldom had time to straighten my back. I had but one thought all day : When will that sun get down to the west ? My neighbour, Jock Tamson, always seemed fresh and cheerful, but, unfortunately, I did not discover the cause of his optimism until the last day.

" Foo are you feenished so quick, Jock ? " I asked.

Jock winked and nodded his head in the direction of the farmer.

" Look ! " he said, and he skilfully tramped a big potato into the earth with his right foot ; then he surreptitiously happed it over with his left.

I have never forgiven Jock for being so tardy in spreading his gospel.

*   *   *

To-day I received from the Clerk the Report on my school.

" Discipline," it says, " which is kindly, might be firmer, especially in the Senior Division, so as to prevent a tendency to talk on the part of the pupils whenever opportunity occurs."

An earlier part runs thus : " The pupils in the Senior Division are intelligent and bright under oral examination, and make an exceedingly good appearance in the class subjects."

I scratch my head thoughtfully. If the inspector finds the bairns intelligent and bright, why does he want them to be silent in school ? I cannot tell ; I suspect that talking children annoy him. I fancy that stern disciplinarians are men who hate to be irritated.

" More attention, however, should be paid to neatness of method and penmanship in copybooks and jotters."

I wonder. I freely admit to myself that the jotters are not neat, but I want to know why they should be. I can beat most men at marring a page with hasty figures ; on the other hand I can make a page look like copperplate if I want to. I find that my bairns do neat work on an examination paper.

The truth is that I am incapable of teaching neatness. My desk is a jumble; my sitting-room is generally littered with books and papers. Some men are born tidy: some have tidiness thrust upon them. I am of the latter crowd. Between the school charwoman and my landlady I live strenuously.

I object to my report. I hate to be the victim of a man I can't reply to, even when he says nice things. But the main objection I have to the report is this: the School Board gets not a single word of criticism. If I were not almost proud of my lack of neatness, I might argue that no man could be neat in an ugly school. It is always filthy because the ashed playground is undrained. Broken windows stand for months; the plaster of the ceiling came down months ago, and the lathes are still showing. The School Board does not worry; its avowed object is to keep down the rates at any price in mean-ness (some members are big ratepayers). The sanitary arrangements are a disgrace to a long-suffering nation. Nothing is done.

* * *

It would be a good plan to make teachers forward reports of inspectors' visits to the

Scotch Education Department.   I should love to write one.

" Mr. Silas K. Beans, H.M.I.S., paid a visit to this school to-day, and he made quite a passable appearance before the pupils.

" It was perhaps unfortunate that Mr. Beans laboured under the delusion that Mrs. Hemans wrote *Come into the Garden, Maud*, but on the whole the subject was adequately treated.

" The geography lesson showed Mr. Beans at his best, but it might be advisable for him to consider whether the precise whereabouts of Seville possesses the importance in the scheme of things that he attributes to it. And it might be suggested that children of twelve find some difficulty in spelling Prsym— Prysem— Pryems——anyway, the name of the town that has kept the alleged comic weeklies alive during a trying period.

" The school staff would have liked Mr. Beans to have stayed long enough to discover that a few of the scholars possessed imagination, and it hoped that he will be able to make his visit longer than four hours next time.

" Mr. Beans's knowledge of dates is wonderful, and his parsing has all the glory of Early Victorian furniture."

XIII.

TO-NIGHT MacMurray invited me down to meet his former head, Simpson, a big man in the Educational Institute, and a likely President next year. Mac introduced me as " a chap with theories on education ; doesn't care a rap for inspectors and abominates discipline."

Simpson looked me over ; then he grunted.

" You'll grow out of that, young man," he said sagely.

I laughed.

" That's what I'm afraid of," I said, " I fear that the continual holding of my nose to the grindstone will destroy my perspective."

" You'll find that experience doesn't destroy perspective."

" Experience," I cried, " is, or at least, should be one of Oscar Wilde's Seven Deadly Virtues. The experienced man is the chap who funks doing a thing because he's had his fingers burnt. 'Tis experience that makes cowards of us all."

" Of course," said Simpson, " you're joking. It stands to reason that I, for instance, with a thirty-four years' experience of teaching know more about education than you do, if you don't mind my saying so."

" Man, I was teaching laddies before your father and mother met," he added.

" If you saw a lad and a lass making love would you arrange that he should sit near her ? "

" Good gracious, no ! " he cried. " What has that got to do with the subject."

" But why not give them chances to spoon? " I asked.

" Why not ? If a teacher encouraged that sort of thing, why, it might lead to anything ! "

" Exactly," I said, " experience tells you that you have to do all you can to preserve the morals of the bairns ? "

" I could give you instances— "

" I don't want them particularly," I interrupted. " My main point is that experience has made you a funk. Pass the baccy, Mac."

" Mean to tell me that's how you teach ? " cried Simpson. " How in all the world do you do for discipline ? "

" I do without it."

" My goodness ! that's the limit ! May I ask why you do without it ? "

" It is a purely personal matter," I answered. " I don't want anyone to lay down definite rules for me, and I refuse to lay down definite rules of conduct for my bairns."

" But how in all the earth do you get any work done ? "

" Work," I said, " is an over-rated thing, just as knowledge is overrated."

" Nonsense," said Simpson.

" All right," I remarked mildly, " if knowledge is so important, why is a university professor usually a talker of platitudes ? Why is the average medallist at a university a man of tenth-rate ideas ? "

" Then our Scotch education is all in vain ? "

" Speaking generally, it is."

I think it was at this stage that Simpson began to doubt my sanity.

" Young man," he said severely, " some day you will realise that work and knowledge and discipline are of supreme importance. Look at the Germans ! "

He waved his hand in the direction of the sideboard, and I looked round hastily.

" Look what Germany has done with work and knowledge and discipline ! "

" Then why all this bother to crush a State that has all the virtues ? " I asked diffidently.

" It isn't the discipline we are trying to crush; it is the militarism."

" Good ! " I cried, " I'm glad to hear it. That's what I want to do in Scotland; I want to crush the militarism in our schools, and, as most teachers call their militarism discipline, I curse discipline."

" That's all rubbish, you know," he said shortly.

" No it isn't.   If I leather a boy for making a mistake in a sum, I am no better than the Prussian officer who shoots a Belgian civilian for crossing the street.   I am equally stupid and a bully."

" Then you allow carelessness to go un-punished ? " he sneered.

" I do.   You see I am a very careless devil myself.   I'll swear that I left your garden gate open when I came in, Mac, and your hens will be all over the road."

Mac looked out at the window.

" They are ! " he chuckled, and I laughed.

" You seem to think that slovenliness is a virtue," said Simpson with a faint smile.

" I don't, really, but I hold that it is a natural human quality."

" Are your pupils slovenly ? " he asked.

" Lots of 'em are. You're born tidy or you aren't."

" When these boys go out to the workshop, what then ?   Will a joiner keep an apprentice who makes a slovenly job ? "

" Ah ! " I said, " you're talking about trade now. You evidently want our schools to turn out practical workmen. I don't. Mind you I'm quite willing to admit that a shoemaker who theorises about leather is a public nuisance. Neatness and skill are necessary in practical manufacture, but I refuse to reduce education to the level of cobbling or coffin-making. I don't care how slovenly a boy is if he thinks."

" If he is slovenly he won't think," said Simpson.

I smiled.

" I think you are wrong. Personally, I am a very lazy man; I have my library all over the floor as a rule. Yet, though I am lazy physically I am not lazy mentally. I

hold that the really lazy teacher is your
" ring the bell at nine sharp" man; he
hustles so much that he hasn't time to think.
If you work hard all day you never have time
to think."

Simpson laughed.

" Man, I'd like to see your school ! "

" Why not ? Come up tomorrow morning,"
I said.

" First rate ! " he cried, " I'll be there at
nine."

" Better not," I said with a smile, " or
you'll have to wait for ten minutes."

* * *

He arrived as I blew the " Fall in " on my
bugle.

" You don't line them up and march them
in ? " he said.

" I used to, but I've given it up," I con-
fessed. " To tell the truth I'm not enamoured
of straight lines."

We entered my classroom. Simpson stood
looking sternly at my chattering family while
I marked the registers.

" I couldn't tolerate this row," he said.

" It isn't so noisy as your golf club on a
Saturday night, is it ? " He smiled slightly.

Jim Burnett came out to my desk and lifted *The Glasgow Herald,* then he went out to the playground humming *On the Mississippi.*

" What's the idea ? " asked Simpson.

" He's the only boy who is keen on the war news," I explained.

Then Margaret Steel came out.

" Please, sir, I took *The Four Feathers* home and my mother began to read them ; she thinks she'll finish them by Sunday. Is anybody reading *The Invisible Man ?* "

I gave her the book and she went out.

Then Tom Macintosh came out and asked for the Manual Room key ; he wanted to finish a boat he was making.

" Do you let them do as they like ? " asked Simpson.

" In the upper classes," I replied.

Soon all the Supplementary and Qualifying pupils had found a novel and had gone out to the roadside. I turned to give the other classes arithmetic.

Mary Wilson in the front seat held out a bag of sweets to me. I took one.

" Please, sir, would the gentleman like one, too ? "

Simpson took one with the air of a man on

holiday who doesn't care what sins he commits.

" I say," he whispered, " do you let them eat in school ? There's a boy in the back seat eating nuts."

I fixed Ralph Ritchie with my eye.

" Ralph ! If you throw any nutshells on that floor Mrs. Findlay will eat you."

" I'm putting them in my pooch," he said.

" Good ! Write down this sum."

" What are the others doing ? " asked Simpson after a time.

" Margaret Steel and Violet Brown are reading," I said promptly. " Annie Dixon is playing fivies on the sand, Jack White and Bob Tosh are most likely arguing about horses, but the other boys are reading, we'll go and see." And together we walked down the road.

Annie was playing fivies all right, but Jack and Bob weren't discussing horses ; they were reading *Chips*.

" And the scamps haven't the decency to hide it when you appear ! " cried Simpson.

" Haven't the fear," I corrected.

On the way back to the school he said : " It's all very pleasant and picnicy, but eating nuts and sweets in class ! "

" Makes your right arm itch ? " I suggested pleasantly.

" It does," he said with a short laugh, " Man, do you never get irritated ? "

" Sometimes."

" Ah ! " He looked relieved. " So the system isn't perfect ? "

" Good heavens ! " I cried, " What do you think I am ? A saint from heaven ? You surely don't imagine that a man with nerves and a temperament is always able to enter into the moods of bairns ! I get ratty occasionally, but I generally blame myself." I sent a girl for my bugle and sounded the " Dismiss."

" What do you do now ? "

I pulled out my pipe and baccy.

" Have a fill," I said, " it's John Cotton."

*　　*　　*

To-night I have been thinking about Simpson. He is really a kindly man ; in the golf-house he is voted a good fellow. Yet Mac-Murray tells me that he is a very strict disciplinarian ; he saw him give a boy six scuds with the tawse one day for drawing a man's face on the inside cover of his drawing book. I suppose that Simpson considers that he is an eminently just man.

I think that the foundation of true justice is self-analysis. It is mental laziness that is at the root of the militarism in our schools. Simpson is as lazy mentally as the proverbial mother who cried: "See what Willie's doing and tell him he musn't." I wonder what he would have replied if the boy had said: "Why is it wrong to draw a man's face in a drawing book?" Very likely he would have given him another six for impertinence.

It is strange that our boasted democracy uses its power to set up bullies. The law bullies the poor and gives them the cat if they trespass; the police bully everyone who hasn't a clean collar; the dominie bullies the young; and the School Board bullies the dominie. Yet, in theory, the judge, the constable, the dominie, and the School Board are the servants of democracy. Heaven protect us from the bureaucratic Socialism of people like the Webbs! It is significant that Germany, the country of the super-official is the country of the super-bully.

Paradoxically, I, as a Socialist, believe that

the one thing that will save the people is
individualism. No democracy can control
a stupid teacher or a stupid judge. If our
universities produce teachers who leather a
boy for drawing a face, and judges who give
boys the cat for stealing tuppence ha'penny,
then our universities are all wrong. Or
human nature is all wrong. If I admit the
latter I must fall back on pessimism. But I
don't admit it. Our cruel teachers and
magistrates are good fellows in their clubs
and homes ; they are bad fellows in their
schools and courts because they have never
come to think, to examine themselves. In
my Utopia self-examination will be the only
examination that will matter.

H. G. Wells in *The New Machiavelli* talks
of " Love and Fine Thinking " as the salvation of the world. I like the phrase, but I
prefer the word Realisation. I want men like
Simpson to realise that their arbitrary rules
are unjust and cowardly and inhuman.

*   *   *

I saw a good fight to-night. At four o'clock
I noticed a general move towards Murray's
Corner, and I knew that blood was about to
be shed. Moreover I knew that Jim Steel

was to tackle the new boy Welsh, for I had seen Jim put his fist to his nose significantly in the afternoon.

I followed the crowd.

" I want to see fair play," I said.

Welsh kept shouting that he could " fecht the hale schule wi' wan hand tied ahent 'is back."

In this district school fights have an etiquette of their own. One boy touches the other on the arm saying : " There's the dunt ! " The other returns the touch with the same remark. If he fails to return it he receives a harder dunt on the arm with the words, " And there's the coordly ! " If he fails to return that also he is accounted the loser, and the small boys throw divots at him.

Steel began in the usual way with his : " There's the dunt ! " Welsh promptly hit him in the teeth and knocked him down. The boys appealed to me.

" No," I said, " Welsh didn't know the rules. After this you should shake hands as you do in boxing."

Welsh never had a chance. He had no science ; he came on with his arms swinging in windmill fashion. Jim stepped aside and drove a straight left to the jaw, and before Welsh knew what was happening Jim landed him on the nose with his right. Welsh began to weep, and I stopped the fight. I told him that Steel had the advantage because I had taught my boys the value of a straight left, but that I would give him a few lessons with the gloves later on. Then I asked how the quarrel had arisen. As I had conjectured Steel and Welsh had no real quarrel. Welsh had cuffed little Geordie Burnett's ears, and Geordie had cried, " Ye wudna hit Jim Steel ! " Welsh had no alternative but to reply : " Wud Aw no ! " Straightway Geordie had run off to Steel saying : " Hi ! Jim ! Peter Welsh says he'll fecht ye ! "

So far as I can remember all my own battles at school were arranged by disobliging little boys in this manner. If Jock Tamson said to me : " Bob Young cud aisy fecht ye and ca' yer nose up among yer hair ! " I, as a man of honour, had to reply : "Aw'll try Bob Young ony day he likes ! " And even if Bob were my bosom friend, I would have to face him at the brig at four o'clock.

I noticed that the girls were all on Steel's

side before the fight began, and obviously
on Welsh's side when he was beaten, the
bissoms !

XIV.

I GAVE a lecture in the village hall on Friday night, and many parents came out to hear what I had to say on the subject of *Children and their Parents.* After the lecture I invited questions.

" What wud ye hae a man do if his laddie wudna do what he was bidden ? " asked Brown the joiner.

" I would have the man think very seriously whether he had any right to give the order that was disobeyed. For instance, if you ordered your Jim to stop singing while you were reading, you would be taking an unfair advantage of your years and size. From what I know of Jim he would certainly stop singing if you asked him to do so as a favour."

" Aw dinna believe in askin' favours o' ma laddies," he said.

I smiled.

" Yet you ask them of other laddies. You don't collar Fred Thomson and shout:

'Post that letter at once!' You say very
nicely: 'You might post that letter like a
good laddie,' and Fred enjoys posting your
letter more than posting a ton of letters for
his own father."

The audience laughed, and Fred's father
cried: "Goad! Ye're quite richt, dominie!"

"As a boy," I continued, "I hated being
set to weed the garden, though I spent hours
helping to weed the garden next door. A
boy likes to grant favours."

"Aye," said Brown, "when there's a
penny at the tail end o' them!"

"Yes," I said after the laughter had died,
"but your Jim would rather have Mr.
Thomson's penny than your sixpence. The
real reason is that you boss your son, and
nobody likes to be bossed."

"Believe me, ladies and gentlemen, I
think that the father is the curse of the home.
(Laughter.) The father never talks to his
son as man to man. As a result a boy
suppresses much of his nature, and if he is
left alone with his father for five minutes he
feels awkward, though not quite so awkward
as the father does. You find among the
lower animals that the father is of no im-

portance ; indeed, he is looked on as a danger. Have you ever seen a bitch flare up when the father comes too near her puppies ? Female spiders, I am told, solve the problem of the father by eating him." (Great laughter.)

" What aboot the mothers ? " said a voice, and the men cackled.

" Mothers are worse," I said. " Fathers usually imagine that they have a sense of justice, but mothers have absolutely no sense of justice. It is the mother who cries, ' Liz, ye lazy slut, run and clean your brother's boots, the poor laddie ! Lod, I dinna ken what would happen to you, my poor laddie, if your mother wasna here to look after you.' You mothers make your girls work at nights and on Saturdays, and you allow your boys to play outside. That is most unjust. Your boys should clean their own boots and mend their own clothes. They should help in the washing of dishes and the sweeping of floors."

" Wud ye say that the mother is the curse o' the hame, too ? " asked Brown.

" No," I said, " she is a necessity, and in spite of her lack of justice, she is nearer to the children than the father is. She is less aloof and less stern. You'll find that a boy will tell his mother much more than he will tell his father. Speaking generally, a stupid mother is more dangerous than a stupid father, but a mother of average intelligence is better for a child than a father of average intelligence.

" This is a problem that cannot be solved. The mother must remain with her children, and I cannot see how we are to chuck the father out of the house. As a matter of fact he is usually so henpecked that he is prevented from being too much of an evil to the bairns.

" The truth is that the parents of to-day are not fit to be parents, and the parents of the next generation will be no better. The mothers of the next generation are now in my school. They will leave at the age of four-teen—some of them will be exempted and leave at thirteen—and they will slave in the fields or the factory for five or six years. Then society will accept them as legitimate guardians of the morals and spiritual welfare of children. I say that this is a damnable system. A mother who has never learned to think has absolute control of a growing young mind, and an almost absolute control of a growing young body. She can beat her child; she can starve it. She can poison its mind with malice, just as she can poison its body with gin and bitters.

"What can we do? The home is the Englishman's castle! Anyway, in these days of high explosives, castles are out of date, and it is high time that the castle called home had some airing."

*   *   *

I cannot flatter myself that I made a single parent think on Friday night. Most of the villagers treated the affair as a huge joke.

I have just decided to hold an Evening School next winter. I see that the Code offers *The Life and Duties of a Citizen* as a subject. I shall have the lads and lasses of sixteen to nineteen in my classroom twice a week, and I guess I'll tell them things about citizenship they won't forget.

It occurs to me that married people are not easily persuaded to think. The village girl considers marriage the end of all things. She dons the bridal white, and at once she rises meteorically in the social scale. Yesterday she was Mag Broon, an outworker at

Millside; to-day she is Mrs. Smith with a house of her own.

Her mental horizon is widened. She can talk about anything now; the topic of child-birth can now be discussed openly with other married wives. Aggressiveness and mental arrogance follow naturally, and with these come a respect for church-going and an abhorrence of Atheism.

I refuse to believe those who prate about marriage as an emancipation for a woman. Marriage is a prison. It shuts a woman up within her four walls, and she hugs all her prejudices and hypocrisies to her bosom. The men who shout "Women's place is the home!" at Suffragette meetings are fools. The home isn't good enough for women.

A girl once said to me: "I always think that marriage makes a girl a 'has been.'"

What she meant was that marriage ended flirtation, poor innocent that she was! Yet her remark is true in a wider sense. The average married woman is a "has been" in thought, while not a few are "never wasers." Hence I have more hope of my evening school lasses than of their mothers. They have not become smug, nor have they concluded that they are past enlightenment. They are not too omniscient to resent the offering of new ideas.

A man's marriage makes no great change in his life. His wife replaces his mother in such matters as cooking and washing and "feeding the brute." He finds that he is allowed to spend less, and he has to keep elders' hours. But in essentials his life is unchanged. He still has his pint on a Saturday night, and his evening crack at the Brig. He has gained no additional authority, and he is extremely blessed of the gods if he has not lost part of the authority he had.

The revolution in his mental outfit comes later when he becomes a father. He thinks that his education is complete when the midwife whispers: "Hi, Jock, it's a lassie!" He immediately realises that he is a man of importance, a guide and preacher rolled into one; and he talks dictatorially to the dominie about education. Then he discovers that precept must be accompanied by example, and he aspires to be a deacon or an elder.

Now I want to get at Jock before the midwife gets at him. I don't care tuppence whether he is married or not....but he mustn't be a father.

*　　*　　*

To-day I began to read Mary Johnston's *By Order of the Company* to my bairns. I love the story, and I love the style. It reminds me of Malory's style; she has his trick of running on in a breathless string of " ands." When I think of style I am forced to recollect the stylists I had to read at the university. There was Sir Thomas Browne and his *Urn Burial.* What the devil is the use of people like Browne I don't know. He gives us word music and imagery I admit, but I don't want word music and imagery from prose, I want ideas or a story. I can't think of one idea I got from Browne or Fisher or Ruskin, or any of the stylists, yet I have found many ideas in translations of Nietzsche and Ibsen. Style is the curse of English literature.

When I read Mary Johnston I forget all about words. I vaguely realise that she is using the right words all the time, but the story is the thing. When I read Browne I fail to scrape together the faintest interest in burials; the organ music of his *Dead March* drowns everything else.

When a man writes too musically and ornately I always suspect him of having a paucity of ideas. If you have anything important to say you use plain language. The man who writes to the local paper complaining of " those itinerant denizens of the underworld yclept hawkers, who make the day hideous with raucous cries," is a pompous ass. Yet he is no worse than the average stylist in writing. I think it was G. K. Chesterton who said that a certain popular authoress said nothing because she believed in words. He might have applied the phrase to 90 per cent of English writers.

Poetry cannot be changed. Substitute a word for " felicity " in the line: " Absent thee from felicity awhile " and you destroy the poetry. But I hold that prose should be able to stand translation. The prose that cannot stand it is the empty stuff produced by our Ruskins and our Brownes. Empty barrels always have made the most sound.

* * *

There must be something in style after all. I had this note from a mother this morning.

" DEAR SIR,

Please change Jane's seat for she brings home more than belongs to her."

I refuse to comment on this work of art.

*   *   *

I must get a cornet. Eurhythmics with an artillery bugle is too much for my wind and my dignity. Just when the graceful bend is coming forward my wind gives out, and I make a vain attempt to whistle the rest. Perhaps a concertina would be better than a cornet. I tried Willie Hunter with his mouth-organ, but the attempt was stale and unprofitable, and incidentally flat. Then Tom Macintosh brought a comb to the school and offered to perform on it. After that I gave Eurhythmics a rest.

When the war is over 1 hope that the Government will retain Lloyd George as Minister of Munitions....for Schools. I haven't got a tenth of the munitions I should have ; I want a player-piano, a gramophone, a cinematograph with comic films, a library with magazines and pictures. I want swings and see-saws in the playground, I want rabbits and white mice ; I want instruments for a school brass and wood band.

I like building castles in Spain. The truth is that if the School Board would yield to my importunities and lay a few loads of gravel on the muddy patch commonly known as the playground I should almost die of surprise and joy. One learns to be content with small mercies when one is serving those ratepayers who control the rates.

XV.

MARGARET STEEL has left school, and to-morrow morning she goes off at five o'clock to the factory.

To-day Margaret is a bright-eyed, rosy-cheeked lassie; in three years she will be hollow-eyed and pale-faced. Never again will she know what it is to waken naturally after sleep; the factory syren will haunt her dreams always. She will rise at half-past four summer and winter; she will tramp the two mile road to the factory, and when six comes at night she will wearily tramp home again. Possibly she will marry a factory worker and continue working in the factory, for his wage will not keep up a home. In the neighbouring town hundreds of homes are locked all day....and Bruce the manufacturer's daughters are in county society. Heigh ho! It is a queer thing civilisation!

I wonder when the people will begin to

realise what wagery means. When they do
begin to realise they will commence the revolution by driving women out of industry.
To-day the women are used by the profiteer
as instruments to exploit the men. Surely
a factory worker has the right to earn enough
to support a family on. The profiteer says
" No ! You must marry one of my hands,
and then your combined wages will set up a
home for you."

I spoke of this to the manager of Bruce's
factory once.

" But," he said, " if we did away with
female labour we'd have to close down. We
couldn't compete with other firms."

" Not if they abolished female labour
too ? "

" I was thinking of the Calcutta mills
where labour is dirt cheap," he said.

" I see," I said, " so the Scotch lassie is
to compete with the native ? "

" It comes to that," he admitted.

I think I see a very pretty problem awaiting
Labour in the near future. As the Trade
Unions become more powerful and show their
determination to take the mines and factories
into their own hands, capitalists will turn

to Asia and Africa. The exploitation of the native is just beginning. At a time when Britain is a Socialistic State all the evils of capitalism will be reproduced with ten-fold intensity in India and China and Africa. I see an Asia ruled by lash and revolver ; the profiteer has a short way with the striker in Eastern climes. The recent history of South Africa is sinister. A few years ago our brothers died presumably that white men should have the rights of citizenship in the Transvaal. What they seemed to have died for was the right of profiteers to shoot white strikers from the windows of the Rand Club. If white men are treated thus I tremble for the fate of the black man who strikes.

Yes, the present profiteering system is a preparation for an exploited East. Margaret Steel and her fellows are slaving so that a Persia may be " opened up," a Mexico robbed of its oil wells.

*   *   *

To-day I gave a lesson on Capital.

" If," I said, " I have a factory I have to pay out wages and money for machinery and raw material. When I sell my cloth I get more money than I paid out. This money is called profit, and with this money I can set up a new factory.

"Now what I want you to understand is this :—Unless work is done by someone there is no wealth. If I make a fortune out of linen I make it by using the labour of your fathers, and the machinery that was invented by clever men. Of course, I have to work hard myself, but I am repaid for my work fully. Margaret Steel at this moment standing at a loom, is working hard too, but she is getting a wage that is miserable.

"Note that the owner of the factory is getting an income of, say, ten thousand pounds a year. Now, what does he do with the money ? "

" Spends it on motor cars," said a boy.

" Buys cigarettes," said a girl.

" Please, sir, Mr. Bruce gives money to the infirmary," said another girl.

" He keeps it in a box beneath the bed," said another, and I found that the majority in the room favoured this theory. This suggestion reminded me of the limitations of childhood, and I tried to talk more simply. I told them of banks and stocks, I talked of luxuries, and pointed out that a man who lived by selling expensive dresses to women was doing unnecessary labour.

Tom Macintosh showed signs of thinking deeply.

" Please, sir, what would all the dressmakers and footmen do if there was no money to pay them ? "

" They would do useful work, Tom," I said. " Your father works from six to six every day, but if all the footmen and chauffeurs and grooms and gamekeepers were doing useful work, your father would only need to work maybe seven hours a day. See ? In Britain there are forty millions of people, and the annual income of the country is twenty-four hundred million pounds. One million of people take half this sum, and the other thirty-nine millions have to take the other half."

" Please, sir," said Tom, " what half are you in ? "

" Tom," I said, " I am with the majority. For once the majority has right on its side."

*   *   *

Bruce the manufacturer had an advertisement in to-day's local paper. " No encum-

brances," says the ad. Bruce has a family
of at least a dozen, and he possibly thinks
that he has earned the right to talk of
" encumbrances." I sympathise with the
old chap.

But I want to know why gardeners and
chauffeurs must have no encumbrances. If
the manorial system spreads, a day will come
when the only children at this school will be
the offspring of the parish minister. Then,
I suppose, dominies and ministers will be
compelled to be polygamists by Act of Parliament.

I like the Lord of the Manor's damned
impudence. He breeds cattle for showing,
he breeds pheasants for slaughtering, he breeds
children to heir his estates. Then he sits
down and pens an advertisement for a slave
without " encumbrances." Why he doesn't
import a few harem attendants from Turkey
I don't know ; possibly he is waiting till the
Dardanelles are opened up.

*   *   *

I have just been reading a few schoolboy
howlers. I fancy that most of these howlers
are manufactured. I cannot be persuaded
that any boy ever defined a lie as " An

abomination unto the Lord but a very present help in time of trouble." Howlers bore me; so do most school yarns. The only one worth remembering is the one about the inspector who was ratty.

" Here, boy," he fired at a sleepy youth, " who wrote *Hamlet ?* "

The boy started violently.

" P—please, sir, it wasna me," he stammered.

That evening the inspector was dining with the local squire.

" Very funny thing happened to-day," he said, as they lit their cigars.

" I was a little bit irritated, and I shouted at a boy, ' Who wrote *Hamlet ?* ' The little chap was flustered. ' P—please, sir, it wasna me ! ' he stuttered."

The squire guffawed loudly.

" And I suppose the little devil had done it after all ! " he roared.

*   *   *

Lawson came down to see me to-night, and as usual we talked shop.

" It's all very well," he said, " for you to talk about education being all wrong. Any idiot can burn down a house that took many

men to build.   Have you got a definite scheme
to put in its place ? "

The question was familiar to me.   I had
had it fired at me scores of times in the days
when I talked Socialism from a soap-box in
Hyde Park.

" I think I have a scheme," I said modestly.
Lawson lay back in his chair.

" Good !   Cough it up, my son ! "

I smoked hard for a minute.

" Well, Lawson, it's like this, my scheme
could only be a success if the economic basis
of society were altered. So long as one
million people take half the national yearly
income you can't have any decent scheme of
education."

" Right O ! " said Lawson cheerfully, " for
the sake of argument, or rather peace, we'll
give you a Utopia where there are no idle
rich.   Fire away ! "

" Good !   I'll talk about the present day
education first.

"Twenty years ago education had one aim—
—to abolish illiteracy.   In consequence the
Three R.'s were of supreme importance.
Nowadays they are held to be quite as important, but a dozen other things have been

placed beside them on the pedestal. Gradually education has come to aim at turning out a man or a woman capable of earning a living. Cookery, Woodwork, Typing, Bookkeeping, Shorthand....all these were introduced so that we should have better wives and joiners and clerks.

"Lawson, I would chuck the whole blamed lot out of the elementary school. I don't want children to be trained to make pea-soup and picture frames, I want them to be trained to think. I would cut out History and Geography as subjects."

"Eh ? " said Lawson.

"They'd come in incidentally. For instance, I could teach for a week on the text of a newspaper report of a fire in New York."

"The fire would light up the whole world, so to speak," said Lawson with a smile.

"Under the present system the teacher never gets under way. He is just getting to the interesting part of his subject when Maggie Brown ups and says, ' Please, sir, it's Cookery now.' The chap who makes a religion of his teaching says ' Damn ! ' very forcibly, and the girls troop out.

"I would keep Composition and Reading

and Arithmetic in the curriculum. Drill and Music would come into the play hours, and Sketching would be an outside hobby for warm days."

" Where would you bring in the technical subjects ? "

" Each school would have a workshop where boys could repair their bikes or make kites and arrows, but there would not be any formal instruction in woodwork or engineering. Technical education would begin at the age of sixteen."

" Six what ? "

" Sixteen.   You see my pupils are to stay at school till they are twenty. You are providing the cash you know. Well, at sixteen the child would be allowed to select any subject he liked. Suppose he is keen on mechanics. He spends a good part of the day in the engineering shop and the drawing room—mechanical drawing I mean.   But the thinking side of his education is still going on. He is studying political economy, eugenics, evolution, philosophy. By the time he is eighteen he has read Nietzsche, Ibsen, Bjornson, Shaw, Galsworthy, Wells, Strindberg, Tolstoi, that is if ideas appeal to him."

" Ah ! "

" Of course, I don't say that one man in a hundred will read Ibsen. You will always have the majority who are averse to thinking if they can get out of it. These will be good mechanics and typists and joiners in many cases. My point is that every boy or girl has the chance to absorb ideas during their teens."

" Would you make it compulsory ? For instance, that boy Willie Smith in your school; do you think that he would learn much more if he had to stay at school till he was twenty ? "

" No," I said, " I wouldn't force anyone to stay at school, but to-day boys quite as stupid naturally as Smith stay at the university and love it. A few years' rubbing shoulders with other men is bound to make a man more alert. Take away, as you have done for argument's sake, the necessity of a boy's leaving school at fourteen to earn a living and you simply make every school a university."

" And it isn't three weeks since I heard you curse universities ! " said Lawson with a grin.

" I'm thinking of the social side of a university," I explained. " That is good. The educational side of our universities is bad because it is mostly cram. I crammed Botany and Zoo for my degree and I know nothing about either ; I was too busy trying to remember words like Caryophylacia, or whatever it is, to ask why flowers droop their heads at night. So in English I had to cram up what Hazlitt and Coleridge said about Shakespeare when I should have been reading *Othello*. The university fails because it refuses to connect education with contemporary life. You go there and you learn a lot of rot about syllogisms and pentameters, and nothing is done to explain to you the meaning of the life in the streets outside. No wonder that Oxford and Cambridge dons write to the papers saying that life has no opening for a university man."

" But I thought that you didn't want education to produce a practical man. You wanted a theoretical chimney-sweep, didn't you ? " said Lawson smiling.

" The present university turns out men who are neither practical nor theoretical. I want a university that will turn out thinkers.

The men who have done most to stimulate thought these past few years are men like Wells and Shaw and Chesterton ; and I don't think that one of them is a ' varsity man.' "

" You can't run a world on thought," said he.

" I don't know," I said, " we seem to run this old State of ours *without* thought. The truth is that there will always be more workers than thinkers. While one chap is planning a new heaven on earth, the other ninety-nine are working hard at motors and benches.

" H. G. Wells is always asking for better technical schools, more research, more invention. All these are absolutely necessary, but I want more than that ; along with science and art I want the thinking part of education to go on."

" It goes on now."

" No," I said, " it doesn't. Your so-called educated man is often a stupid fellow. Doctors have a good specialist education, yet I know a score of doctors who think that Socialism means ' The Great Divide.' When Osteopathy came over from America a few years ago thousands of medical men pronounced it ' damned quackery ' at once; only a few were wide enough to study the thing to see what it was worth. So with inoculation; the doctors follow the antitoxin authority like sheep. At the university I once saw a raid on an Anti-Vivisection shop, and I'm sure that not one medical student in the crowd had ever thought about vivisection. Mention Women's Freedom to the average lawyer, and he will think you a madman.

" Don't you see what I am driving at ? I want first-class doctors and engineers and chemists, but I want them to think also, to think about things outside their immediate interests. This is the age of the specialist. That's what's wrong with it. Somebody, Matthew Arnold, I think, wanted a man who knew everything of something and something of everything. It's a jolly good definition of education."

" That is the idea of the Scotch Code," said Lawson.

" Yes, perhaps it is. They want our bairns to learn tons of somethings about everything that doesn't matter a damn in life."

*   *   *

My talk with Lawson last night makes me realise again how hopeless it is to plan a system of education when the economic system is all out of joint. I believe that this nation has the wealth to educate its children properly. I wonder what the Conscriptionists would say if I hinted to them that if a State can afford to take its youth away from industry to do unprofitable labour in the army and navy it can afford to educate its youth till the age of twenty is reached.

The stuff we teach in school leads nowhere; the Code subjects simply lull a child to sleep. How the devil is a lad to build a Utopia on Geography and Nature Study and Woodwork? Education should prove that the world is out of joint, and it should point a Kitchener finger at each child and say, " Your Country Needs *You*....to set it Right."

XVI.

THIS has been a delightful day. About eleven o'clock a rap came at the door, and a young lady entered my class-room.

"Jerusalem!" I gasped. "Dorothy! Where did you drop from?"

"I'm motoring to Edinburgh," she explained, "on tour, you know, old thing!"

Dorothy is an actress in a musical comedy touring company, and she is a very old friend of mine. She is a delightful child, full of fun and mischief, yet she can be a most serious lady on occasion.

She looked at my bairns, then she clasped her hands.

"O, Sandy! Fancy you teaching all these kiddies! Won't you teach me, too?" And she sat down beside Violet Brown. I thanked my stars that I had never been dignified in that room.

"Dorothy," I said severely, "you're talking to Violet Brown and I must give you the strap."

The bairns simply howled, and when Dorothy took out her wee handkerchief and pretended to cry, laughter was dissolved in tears.

It was minutes time, and she insisted on blowing the " Dismiss " on the bugle. Her efforts brought the house down. The girls refused to dismiss, they crowded round Dorothy and touched her furs. She was in high spirits.

" You know, girls, I'm an actress and this big bad teacher of yours is a very old pal of mine. He isn't such a bad sort really, you know," and she put her arm round my shoulders.

" See her little game, girls ? " I said. " Do you notice that this woman from a disreputable profession is making advances to me ? She really wants me to kiss her, you know. She— " But Dorothy shoved a piece of chalk into my mouth.

What a day we had ! Dorothy stayed all day, and by four o'clock she knew all the big girls by their Christian names. She insisted on their calling her Dorothy. She even tried to talk their dialect, and they screamed at her attempt to say " Guid nicht the noo."

In the afternoon I got her to sing and play ; then she danced a ragtime, and in a few minutes she had the whole crowd ragging up and down the floor.

She stayed to tea, and we reminisced about London. Dear old Dorothy ! What a joy it was to see her again, but how dull will school be tomorrow ! Ah, well, it is a workaday world, and the butterflies do not come out every day. If Dorothy could read that sentence she would purse up her pretty lips and say, " Butterfly, indeed, you old bluebottle ! " The dear child !

*   *   *

The school to-day was like a ballroom the " morning after." The bairns sat and talked about Dorothy, and they talked in hushed tones as about one who is dead.

" Please, sir," asked Violet, " will she come back again ? "

" I'm afraid not," I answered.

" Please, sir, you should marry her, and then she'll always be here."

" She loves another man, Vi," I said ruefully, and when Vi whispered to Katie Farmer, " What a shame ! " I felt very sad. For the moment I loved Dorothy, but it was mere sentimentalism; Dorothy and I could never love, we are too much of the pal to each other for emotion to enter.

" She is very pretty," said Peggy Smith.

" Very," I assented.

" P—please, sir, you—you could marry her if you really tried ? " said Violet. She had been thinking hard for a bit.

" And break the other man's heart ! " I laughed.

Violet wrinkled her brows.

" Please, sir, it wouldn't matter for him, we don't know him."

" Why ! " I cried, " he is a very old friend of mine ! "

" Oh ! " Violet gasped.

" Please, sir," she said after a while, " do you know any more actresses ? "

I seized her by the shoulders and shook her.

" You wee bissom ! You don't care a rap about me ; all you want is that I should marry an actress. You want my wife to come and

teach you ragtimes and tangoes!" And she
blushed guiltily.

*   *   *

Lawson came down to see me again to-
night; he wanted to tell me of an inspector's
visit to-day.

"Why don't you apply for an inspector-
ship?" he asked.

I lit my pipe.

"Various reasons, old fellow," I said.
"For one thing I don't happen to know a
fellow who knows a chap who lives next door
to a woman whose husband works in the
Scotch Education Department.

"Again, I'm not qualified; I never took
the Education Class at Oxford."

"Finally, I don't want the job."

"I suppose," said Lawson, "that lots of
'em get in by wire-pulling."

"Very probably, but some of them probably
get in straight. Naturally, you cannot get
geniuses by wire-pulling; the chap who
uses influence to get a job is a third-rater
always."

Lawson reddened.

"I pulled wires to get into my job," he
said.

" That's all right," I said cheerfully, " I've pulled wires all my days."

" But," I added, " I wouldn't do it again."

" Caught religion ? "

" Not quite. The truth is that I have at last realised that you never get anything worth having if you've got to beg for it."

" It's about the softest job I know, whether you have to beg for it or not. The only job that beats it for softness is the kirk," he said.

" I wouldn't exactly call it a soft job, Lawson ; a rotten job, yes, but a soft job, no. Inspecting schools is half spying and half policing. It isn't supposed to be you know, but it is. You know as well as I do that every teacher starts guiltily whenever the inspector shoves his nose into the room. Nosing, that's what it is."

" You would make a fairly decent inspector," said Lawson.

" Thanks," I said, " the insinuation being that I could nose well, eh ? "

" I didn't mean that. Suppose you had to examine my school how would you do it ? "

" I would come in and sit down on a bench and say : 'Just imagine I am a new boy, and give me an idea of the ways of the school.   I warn you that my attention may wander. Fire away! But, I say, I hope you don't mind my finishing this pie; I had a rotten breakfast this morning.'"

" Go on," said Lawson laughing.

" I wouldn't examine the kids at all. When you let them out for minutes I would have a crack with you. I would say something like this: 'I've got a dirty job, but I must earn my screw in some way. I want to have a wee lecture all to myself. In the first place I don't like your discipline. It's inhuman to make kids attend the way you do. The natural desire of each boy in this room was to watch me put myself outside that pie, and not one looked at me.

" 'Then you are far too strenuous. You went from Arithmetic to Reading without a break. You should give them a five minutes chat between each lesson. And I think you have too much dignity. You would never think of dancing a ragtime on this floor, would you? I thought not. Try it, old chap. Apart from its merits as an antidote to dignity it is a first-rate liver stimulator.' Hello! Where are you going? Time to take 'em in again?

"'O, I say, I'm your guest, uninvited guest, I admit, but that's no reason why you should take advantage of me. Man, my pipe isn't half smoked, and I have a cigarette to smoke yet. Come out and watch me play footer with the boys.'"

"You think you would do all that," said Lawson slowly, "but you wouldn't you know. I remember a young inspector who came into my school with a blush on his face. 'I'm a new inspector,' he said very gingerly, 'and I don't know what I am supposed to do.' A year later that chap came in like whirlwind, and called me 'young man.' Man, you can't escape becoming smug and dignified if you are an inspector."

"I'd have a darned good try, anyway," I said. "Getting any eggs just now?"

* * *

To-night I have been glancing at *The Educational News*. There is a letter in it about inspectors, it is signed "Disgusted." That pseudonym damns the teaching profession utterly and irretrievably. Again and again letters appear, and very seldom does a teacher sign his own name. Naturally, a letter signed with a pseudonym isn't worth reading, for a moral coward is no authority on inspectors or anything else. It sickens me to see the abject cringing cowardice of my fellow teachers. "Disgusted" would no doubt defend himself by saying, "I have a wife and family depending on me and I simply can't afford to offend the inspector."

I grant that there is no point in making an inspector ratty, or for that matter making anyone ratty. I don't advise a man to seize every opportunity for a scrap. There is little use in arguing with an inspector who has methods of arithmetic different to your methods; it is easier to think over his advice and reject it if you are a better arithmetician than he. But if a man feels strongly enough on a subject to write to the papers about it, he ought to write as a man not as a slave. Incidentally, the habit of using a pseudonym damns the inspectorate at the same time. For this habit is universal, and teachers must have heard tales of the victimising of bold writers. Most educational papers suggest by their contributed articles that the teachers of Britain are like a crowd of Public School boys who fear to send their erotic verses to

the school magazine lest the Head flays
them.   No wonder the social status of teachers
is low ; a profession that consists of " Disgusted " and " Rural School " and " Vindex "
and their kind is a profession of nonentities.

*   *   *

Once in my palmy days I told a patient
audience of Londoners that the Post Office
was a Socialist concern.

" Any profits go to the State," I said.

A postman in the crowd stepped forward
and told me what his weekly wage was, and
I hastily withdrew my statement.   To-day
I should define it as a State Concern run on
the principles of Private Profiteering, *i.e.*, it
considers labour a commodity to be bought.

The School Board here is theoretically a
Socialistic body.   Its members are chosen by
the people to spend the public money on
education.   No member can make a profit
out of a Board deal.   Yet this board perpe-
trates all the evils of the private profiteer.

Mrs. Findlay gets ten pounds a year for
cleaning the school.   To the best of my knowledge she works four or five hours a day, and
she spends the whole of each Saturday morning cleaning out the lavatories.   This sum

works out at about sixpence a day or three ha'pence an hour. Most of her work consists of carrying out the very considerable part of the playground that the bairns carry in on their boots. Yet all my requests for a few loads of gravel are ignored.

The members do not think that they are using sweated labour; they say that if Mrs. Findlay doesn't do it for the money half a dozen widows in the village will apply for the job. They believe in competition and the market value of labour.

A few Saturdays ago I rehearsed a cantata in the school, and I offered Mrs. Findlay half a crown for her extra trouble in sweeping the room twice. She refused it with dignity, she didn't mind obliging me, she said. And this kindly soul is merely a " hand " to be bought at the lowest price necessary for subsistence.

Sometimes I curse the Board as a crowd of exploiters, but in my more rational moments I see that they could not do much better if they tried. If Mrs. Findlay had a pound a week the employees of the farmers on the Board would naturally object to a woman's getting a pound a week out of the public funds for working four hours a day while they slaved from sunrise to sunset for less than a pound. A public conscience can never be better than the conscience of the public's representatives. Hence I have no faith in Socialism by Act of Parliament; I have no faith in municipalisation of trams and gas and water. Private profit disappears when the town council takes over the trams, but the greater evil—exploitation of labour remains.

Ah! I suddenly recollect that Mrs. Findlay has her old age pension each Friday. She thus has eight and six a week. I wonder did Lloyd George realise that his pension scheme would one day prevent fat farmers from having conscience qualms when they gave a widow sixpence a day?

*　　*　　*

As I came along the road this morning I saw half a dozen carts disgorging bricks on one of Lappiedub's fields. Lappiedub himself was standing by, and I asked him what was happening.

"Man," he cried lustily, "they've fund coal here and they're to sink pits a' ower the countryside."

When I reached the school the bairns were waiting to tell me the news.

" Please, sir," said Willie Ramsay, " they're going to build a town here bigger than London."

" Bigger than Glasgow even," said Peter Smith.

A few navvies went past the school.

" They're going to build huts for thousands of navvies," said a lassie.

" Please, sir, they'll maybe knock down the school and have a mine here," suggested Violet Brown.

" They won't," I said firmly, " this ugly school will stand until the countryside becomes as ugly as itself. Poor bairns! You don't know what you're coming to. In three years this bonny village will be a smoky blot on God's earth like Newcastle. Dirty women will gossip at dirty doors. You, Willie, will become a miner, and you will walk up that road with a black face. You, Lizzie, will be a trollop of a wife living in a brick hovel. You can hardly escape."

" Mr. Macnab of Lappiedub will lose all his land," said a boy.

" He didn't seem sad when I saw him this morning," I remarked.

" Maybe he's tired of farming," suggested a girl.

" Perhaps," I said, " if he is he doesn't need to worry about farming.   He will be a million-aire in a few years.   He will get a royalty on every ton of coals that comes up from the pit, and he will sit at home and wait for his money.   Simply because he is lucky he will be kept by the people who buy the coals. If he gets sixpence a ton your fathers will pay sixpence more on every ton.   I want you to realise that this is sheer waste.   The men who own the mines will take big profits and keep up big houses with servants and idle daughters.   Then Mr. Macnab will have his share.   Then a man called a middleman will buy the coals and sell them to coal merchants in the towns, and he will have his share. And these men will sell them to the house-holders.   When your father buys his ton of coals he is paying for these things :—the coalowner's income, Mr. Macnab's royalty, the middleman's profit, the town coal mer-chant's profit, and the miners' wages.   If the miners want more wages and strike, they will

get them, but these men won't lose their
profits; they will increase the price of coals
and the householders will pay for the increase.

" Don't run away with the idea that I am
calling Mr. Macnab a scoundrel. He is a
decent, honest, good-natured man who
wouldn't steal a penny from anyone. It isn't
his fault or merit that he is to be rich, it is
the system that is bad."

Thomas Hardy somewhere talks about
" the ache of modernism." I adapt the
phrase and talk about the ache of industrial-
ism. I look out at my wee window and I see
the town that will be. There will be gin
palaces and picture houses and music-halls—
none of them bad things in themselves, but
in a filthy atmosphere they will be hideous
tawdry things with horrid glaring lights. I
see rows of brick houses and acres of clay
land littered with bricks and stones thrown
down any way. Stores will sell cheap boots
and frozen meat and patent pills, packmen
will lug round their parcels of shoddy and
sheen. And education ! They will erect a
new school with a Higher Grade department,
and the Board will talk of turning out the
type of scholar the needs of the community

require. They will have for Rector a B.Sc., and technical instruction will be of first importance. When that happens I shall trek inland and shall seek some rural spot where I can be of some service to the community. I might be able to stand the smoke and filth, but before long there would be a labour candidate for the burgh, and I couldn't stand hearing him spout.

XVII.

I have been considering the subject of school magazines, and I wonder whether it would be possible to run a school magazine here. I have had no experience with a school magazine, but I edited a university weekly for a year. It wasn't a success. I wrote yellow editorials and placarded the quadrangles with flaring bills which screamed " Liars ! " " Are School Teachers Socially Impossible ? " " The Peril and the Pity of the Princes Street Parade," at the undergraduates passing by. It was of no use. No one bothered to reply to my philippics, and I had to sit down and write scathing replies to my own articles. I could never bring my circulation up to the watermark of a previous editor who had written editorials on such bright topics as " The Medical Congress " and " The Work of the International Academic Committee."

In Edinburgh the students are indifferent to their 'varsity magazine, but in St. Andrews the publication of *College Echoes* is the event of the week. The reason is that the St. Andrew's students form a small happy family ; if a reference is made to Bejant Smith everyone understands it. If you mentioned Bejant Smith in the Edinburgh *Student* no one would know whom you were referring to.

The success of *College Echoes* gives me the idea of a school magazine that would succeed. A magazine for my hundred and fifty bairns would be useless ; what I want is a magazine for parents and children. It would be issued weekly, and would mingle school gossip with advice. If Willie Wilson knew that Friday's edition might contain a paragraph to the effect that he had been discovered murdering two young robins, I fancy that he would think twice before he cut their heads off.

I imagine entries like the following :—

" Peter Thomson said on Thursday that it was Lloyd George who said ' Father, I cannot tell a lie,' and he was caned by the master who, by the way, has just been appointed President of the Conservative Association."

" Mary Brown was late every morning this week."

" John Mackenzie is at present gathering potatoes at Mr. Skinnem's farm, and is being paid a shilling a day of ten hours. Mr. Skinnem has been made an elder of the Parish Kirk."

Someone has said that the most arresting piece of literature is your own name in print. That is true, although I suppose that the thrill wears off when you become as public as Winston Churchill or Charlie Chaplin. Why shouldn't the bairns experience this thrill ? When I write the report of a local concert for the local papers I always give prominence to the children who performed. Incidentally, when I have sung at a concert I omit all reference to my part ; I hate to remind the audience that I sang. I am a true altruist in both cases.

Publicity is the most pleasing thing in life, and that's why patent medicines retain their popularity. At present the village cobbler is figuring in the local paper as a " Cured by Bunkum's Bilious Backache Bunion Beans " example, and beneath his photograph (taken at the age of nineteen ; he is fifty-four now) is a glowing testimonial which begins with these words :—" For over a decade I have suffered from an excess of Uric Acid, from Neurotic Dyspepsia, and from Optical Derangements. Until I discovered that marvellous panacea...."

I marvel at his improved literary style; it is only a month since he wrote me as follows :—" Sir, i will be oblidged if you will let peter away at three oclock tonight hoping that you are well as this leaves me i am your obidt servent peter Macannish."

The magazine would also contain interesting editorials for the parents. Art would have a prominent place; if a bairn made a good sketch or a bonny design it would be reproduced.

Of course, the idea cannot be carried out for lack of funds. Yet I fancy that the money now spent on hounds and pet dogs would easily run a magazine for every school in Scotland.

The technical difficulties could easily be overcome. The bigger bairns could read the proofs and paste up the magazine, and the teachers would revise it before sending it to the printers.

I must get estimates from the printers, and

if they are moderate I shall try to raise funds
by giving a school concert.

* 　 * 　 *

I see that the Educational Institute is
advertising for a man who will combine the
post of Editor of *The Educational News* with
the office of Secretary to the Institute. The
salary is £450 per annum.

This combining of the offices seems to me
a great mistake. For an editor should be
a literary man with ideas on education, while
a good secretary should be an organizer.
Because a man can write columns on education, that is no proof that he is the best man
to write to the office washerwoman telling
her not to come on Monday because it is a
holiday.

I could edit the paper (I would take on the
job for a hundred a year and the sport of
telling the other fellow that his notions of
education were all wrong), but I couldn't
organise a party of boys scouts. Kitchener
is a great organiser, but I shouldn't care for
the editorials of *The New Statesman* if he were
editor.

I think that the Institute does not want a

man with ideas. It wants a man who will
mirror the opinions of the Institute. To do
this is a work of genius, for the Institute has
no opinions. No man can represent a body
of men. Suppose the Institute decides by
a majority that it will support the introduction
of " Love " as a subject of the curriculum.
The editor may be a misogynist, or he may
have been married eight times, yet the poor
devil has to sit down and write an editorial
beginning: " Love has too long been absent
from our schools. Who does not remember
with holy tenderness his first kiss ?...."

A paper can be a force only when it is edited
by a man of force and personality. A man
who writes at the dictation of another is a
tenth-rater. That, of course, is why our
press says nothing.

*   *   *

Little Mary Brown was stung by a wasp
the other day as she sat in the class.

" Henceforward," I said, " the wasp that
enters this room is to be slain. Tom Macintosh I appoint you commander in chief."

I begin to think that I prefer the wasp to
the campaign against it. To-day I was in the

midst of a dissertation on Trusts when Tom
started up.

" Come on lads, there's a wasp ! "

They broke a window and two pens ; then
they slew the wasp.

The less studious boys keep one eye on the
window all day, and I found Dave Thomson
chasing an imaginary wasp all round the room
at Arithmetic time. Dave detests Arithmetic. But when I found that Tom Macintosh was smearing the inside window-sill
with black currant jam, I disbanded the anti-
wasp army.

*   *   *

The Inspectors refuse to allow teachers to
use slates nowadays on the ground that they
are insanitary.

To-day I reintroduced slates to all classes.
My one reason was that my bairns were
missing one of the most delightful pastimes
of youth—the joy of making a spittle run
down the slate and back again. I always
look back with tenderness to my old slate.
It was such a serviceable article. By running
my slate-pencil up it I got all the beats of a
drum ; its wooden sides were the acknowledged tests for a new knife, as a hammer it

had few rivals. Then you could play at
X–es and O–ies with impunity; you simply
licked your palm and rubbed the whole game
out when the teacher approached.

In the afternoon half a dozen bairns brought
sponges, and I sighed for the good old days
when sanitary authorities were plumbers on
promotion.

*   *   *

I have given my bairns two songs—
Screw-Guns and *Follow Me Home*, both by
Kipling. I prefer them to the usual " patriotic " song that is published for school use.
I don't see the force of teaching children to be
patriotic; the man who imagines that a
dominie can teach a bairn to love his neighbour or his country is fatuous. Flag-waving
is the last futility of noble minds. The
queer thing is that all these titled men who
spout about Imperialism and Patriotism,
and " Make the Foreigner Pay " are enemies
of the worker. They don't particularly want
to see a State where slums and slavery will
be no more; they are so busy thinking out
a scheme to extend the Empire abroad that
they haven't time to think about the Empire

at home. What is the use of an India or a
South Africa if East Ham is to remain ?

No, I refuse to teach my bairns to sing,
" Britons never, never, never shall be slaves."
My sense of humour won't allow me to
introduce that song.

Although I like Kipling's verses I abominate Kipling's philosophy and politics. He
is always to be found on the same platform
with the Curzons and Milners and Roose-
velts. He believes in " the big stick "; to
him Britain is great because of her financiers,
her viceroys, her engineers. He glories in
enterprise and big ships. He believes with
the late Lord Roberts that the Englishman
is the salt of the earth. I should define
Kipling as a Grown-up Public School Boy.

I always think that the " Patriot's " main
contention is that a man ought to be ready
to die for his country. I freely grant that it
is a great thing to die for your country, but
I contend that it is still greater to live for
your country; and the man who tries to live
for his country usually earns the epithet
" Traitor."

" What do they know of England who
only England know ? " Kipling says this,

or words to this effect. That's the worst of
these travelled Johnnies; they go out to
India or Africa, and two months after their
arrival they pity the narrow vision of the
people at home. After having talked much to
travelled men I have come to the conclusion
that travel is the most narrowing thing on
earth.

" If I went out to India," I remarked one
day to an Anglo-Indian friend at College,
" and if I started to talk about Socialism in
a drawing-room, what would happen ? "

" Oh," he said with a smile, " they would
listen to you very politely, but, of course,
you wouldn't be asked again."

When I went down to Tilbury to see this
friend off to India I looked at the crowd on
the first-class deck.

" Dick," I said, " these people are awful.
Look at their smugness, their eagerness to be
correct at any expense. They are saying
good-bye to wives and mothers and sweethearts, and the whole blessed crowd of 'em
haven't an obvious emotion among 'em. I'll
bet my hat that they won't even wave
their hands when the tender goes off."

As I left the boat the first-class passengers

stood like statues, but one fat woman, with a delightfully plebeian face cried : " So long, old sport ! " to a man beside me.

" Good ! " cried Dick to me with a laugh.

" Lovely ! " I called, and waved my hat frantically to the fat woman. Poor soul, I fear that society out East will be making her suffer for her lapse into bad form.

Travel is like a school-history reader ; it forces you to study mere incident. The travelled man is an encyclopædia of information ; but I don't want to know what a man has seen ; I want to know what he has thought. I am certain that if I went to live in Calcutta I should cease to think. I should marvel at the colour and life of the streets ; I should find great pleasure in learning the lore of the native. But in a year I should very probably be talking of " damned niggers," and cursing the India Office as a crowd of asses who know nothing about India and its problems.

I once lent *Ann Veronica* to a clever young lady. Her father, an engineer who had been all over the world, picked up the book. Two days later he returned it with a final note dismissing me as a dangerous character for his daughter to know. The lady was clever, and had mentality enough to read anything with impunity.

No, travel doesn't broaden a man's outlook.

My writing is like my teaching, it is an irresponsible ramble. I meant to write about songs all the time to-night.

I curse my luck in not being a pianist. I want to give my bairns that loveliest of tenor solos—the *Preislied* from *The Meistersingers*. I want to give them Lawrence Hope's *Slave's Song* from her *Indian Love Lyrics*—" Less than the Dust beneath thy Chariot Wheel." And there are one or two catchy bits in *Gipsy Love* and *The Quaker Girl* that I should like them to know. I am sure that they would enjoy *Mr. Jeremiah, Esquire*, and *The Gipsy's Song*.

XVIII.

THE essay I set to-day was this:—
" Imagine that you are an old lady
who ordered a duck from Gamage's,
and imagine that they sent you an aeroplane
in a crate by mistake. Then describe in the
first person the feelings of the aviator who
found the duck awaiting him at breakfast
time."

One girl wrote :—" Dear Mr. Gamage, I
have not opened the basket, but it seems to
be an ostrich that you have sent. What will
I feed it on ? "

A boy, as the aviator, wrote : " If you
think I am going to risk my life on the machine
you sent you are wrong. It hasn't got a
petrol tank."

The theme was too difficult for the bairns ;
they could not see the ludicrous side. I don't
think one of them visualised the poor old
woman gazing in dismay on the workmen
unloading the crate. H. M. Bateman would

have made an excellent drawing of the incident.

I tried another theme.

"A few days ago I gave you a ha'penny each," I said. "Write a description of how you spent it, and I'll give sixpence to the one who tells the biggest lie."

I got some tall yarns. One chap bought an aeroplane and torpedoed a Zeppelin with it ; one girl bought a thousand motor-cars But Jack Hood, the dunce of the class, wrote these words : "I took it to the church on sunday and put it in the clecshun bag."

I gave him the tanner, although I knew that he had won it by accident. I don't think that Jack will ever get so great a surprise again in this life.

*   *   *

We rambled out to sketch this afternoon. It was very hot, and we lay down under a tree and slept for half-an-hour. Suddenly Violet Brown started up.

"Here's Antonio !" she cried, and the Italian drew his van to the side of the road.

"A slider for each of us," I said, and he began to hustle. My turn came last.

"You like a glass, zir, instead of a zlider?" said Antonio.

"Yes," I replied, "a jolly good suggestion; I haven't had the joy of licking an ice-cream glass dry for many a long day."

It was glorious.

On the way back a girl bought sweets at the village shop. She gave me one.

"Please, sir, it's one of them changing kind," she said.

"Eh?" I hastily took it out and looked at it.

"By George, so it is, Katie!" I cried, "I thought they were dead long since." It was white at first but it changed to blue, then red, then green, then purple. Unfortunately, I bit it unthinkingly, and I never discovered its complete spectrum.

I call this a lucky day; ice cream and changing balls in one afternoon are the quintessence of luck. But man is insatiable; to-night I have a great craving for a stick of twisted sugarelly—the polite call it liquorice.

*   *   *

A couple of Revivalists came to the village a week ago, and they have made a few converts. One of them stopped me on the road to-night and asked if I were saved.

" I am, or, at least, was, a journalist," I said, and walked on chuckling. Of course he gaped, for he did not know why I chuckled. I was thinking of the reporter sitting in the back seat at a Salvationist Meeting. A Salvation lass bent over him. " Are you saved, my friend ? " she whispered. He looked up in alarm.

" I'm a journalist," he said hastily.

" O ! I beg your pardon," she said, and moved on.

I don't like Revivalism. A couple of preachers came to our village when I was a lad, and for a month I thought of nothing but hell. " Only believe ! " one of them used to say when he met you on the road ; the other one had a shorter salutation : " Glory ! " he shouted at you fiercely. Incidentally, the village was a hotbed of petty strife when they departed. And the young women who had stood up to give their " Testimony " were back to the glad-eye phase again within three weeks.

Lizzie Jane Gunn was a typical convert. Lizzie Jane used to describe the night of her

testimony - giving thus :—" Mind you, Aw
was gaein' alang the road, and Aw had just
been gieing ma testimony, and it was gye
dark and Aw was by ma leensome. Weel,
a' at eence something fell into ma hand, and
Aw thocht that it was a message frae the
Loard ; so Aw just grippit ma hand ticht,
an' Aw didna look to see fat it wuz. Fan
Aw got hame Aw lookit to see fat wuz in ma
hand, an' d'ye ken fat it wus ?....a button
aff ma jaicket ! "

I have no sympathy with all this " saving "
business. It's a cowardly selfish religion that
makes people so anxious about their tuppence-
ha'penny souls. When I think of all the
illiterate lay preachers I have listened to I
feel like little Willie at the Sunday School.

"Hands up all those who would like to
go to Heaven !" said the teacher. Willie
alone did not put his hand up.

"What ! Mean to tell me, Willie, that
you don't want to go to Heaven ? "

Willie jerked a contemptuous thumb towards the others.

"No bloomin' fear," he muttered, "not
if that crowd's goin'."

Shelley says that "most wretched men

are cradled into poetry through wrong."
I think that most wretched preachers are
cradled into preaching through conceit. It
is thrilling to have an audience hang upon
your words ; we all like the limelight. Usually
we have to master a stiff part before we can
face the audience. Preaching needs no preparation, no thinking, no merit ; all you do
is to stand up and say : " Deara friendsa,
when I was in the jimmynasium at Peebles,
a fellow lodger of mine blasphemeda. From
that daya, deara friendsa, that son of the
devila nevera prospereda. O, friendsa ! If
you could only looka into your evila heartsa.
...."

I note that when Revivalists come to a
village the so-called village lunatic is always
among the first to give his testimony. Willie
Baffers has been whistling *Life, Life, Eternal
Life* all the week, but I was glad to note that
he was back to *Stop yer Ticklin', Jock*, to-
night.

*   *   *

I have introduced two new text-books—
Secret Remedies, and *More Secret Remedies*.
These books are published by the British

Medical Association at a shilling each, and they give the ingredients and cost of popular patent medicines.

These books should be in every school. Everyone should know the truth about these medicines, and unless our schools tell the truth, the public will never know it. No daily newspaper would think of giving the truth, for the average daily is kept alive by patent medicine advertisements.

I marvel at the mentality of the man who can sell a farthing's worth of drugs for three and sixpence. I don't blame the man ; I merely marvel at him. What is his standard of truth ? What does he imagine the purpose of life to be ?

Poor fellow ! I fancy he is a man born with a silver knife in his mouth, as Chesterton says in another context ; either that, or he is born poor in worldly goods and in spirit. He is dumped down in an out-of-joint world where money and power are honoured, where honesty is never the best policy ; the poor, miserable little grub realises that he has not the ability to earn money or power honestly; but he knows that people are fools, and that a knave always gets the better of a fool.

Our laws are really funny. I can swindle
thousands by selling a nostrum, but if I sign
Andrew Carnegie's name on a cheque I am
sent to Peterhead Prison. Britain is in-
dividualistic to the backbone. The individual
must be protected, but the crowd can look
after itself. If I steal a pair of boots and
run for it, I am a base thief ; if I turn bookie
and become a welsher I have entered the
higher realms of sport, and I get a certain
amount of admiration....from those who
didn't plunge at my corner. I have seen
a cheap-jack swindle a crowd of Forfarshire
ploughmen out of a month's earnings, but
not one of them thought of dusting the street
with him.

Honesty must be a relative thing. Personally I will " swick " a railway company
by travelling without a ticket on any possible
occasion ; yet, when a cycle agent puts a
new nut on my motor-bike and charges a
shilling I call him a vulgar thief. Of course
he is ; there is no romance in making a
broken-down motor-cyclist pay through the
nose, but a ten mile journey without a ticket
is the only romantic experience left in a drab
world.

I once saw an article on *Railway Criminals* in, I think, *Tit-Bits*. It pointed out that the men who are convicted of swindling the railway companies have well marked facial characteristics   I recollect going to the mirror at the time and saying " Tu quoque ! "

In these days I had a firm belief in physiognomy ; I believed that you had only to gaze into a person's eyes to see whether he was telling the truth or not. I am wiser now that I know Peter Young. Pete is ten, and he has a clear, honest countenance. To-night I found him tinkering with the valve of my back tyre.

" Who loosened that valve ? " I demanded.

" Please, sir, it was Jim Steel," he said un-blushingly, and he looked me straight in the eyes.

" All right, George Washington," I re-marked. " There's a seat in the Cabinet, waiting for you, my lad." And I meant it too. I believe in the survival of the fittest, and I know that Peter is the best adapted to survive in a modern civilisation. It is said of his father that he bought an old woman's ill-grown pig, a white one, and pro-mised her a fine piebald pig in a week's

time. He brought her the piebald. Then
rain came....

I often condemn the press for not seeking
truth, yet no man has a greater admiration for a good liar than I have. When I
hear a fellow break in on a conversation with
the words : " Talking of Lloyd George, when
I was in the Argentine last winter...." I
grapple him to my soul with hoops of steel.
I can't stand the common or garden liar
with his trite expressions...." So the missis
is keeping better, old man ? Glad to hear
it." " Your singing has improved wonder-
fully, my dear." " I was kept late at the
office," and all that sort of lie. All the same
I recognise that we are all liars, and few of
us can evade the trite manner of lying.

I met a man on the road to-night, and he
stopped to talk. I hate the fellow ; he is
one of those mean men who would plant
potatoes on his mother's grave if the cemetery
authorities would allow it. Yet I shook his
greasy hand when he held it out. If I had
had the tense honesty of Ibsen's *Brand* I
should have refused to see his hand. But
we all lie in this way ; indeed, life would be
intolerable if we were all *Brands* and cried

"All or Nothing!" We all compromise, and compromise is the worst lie of all. Compromise I can pardon, but not gush. I know men who could say to old greasy-fist: "Man, I'm glad to see you looking so well!" men who would cut his throat if they had the pluck. Nevertheless gush is not one of the Scot's chief characteristics.

There is a shepherd's hut up north, and George Broon lives there alone. Once another shepherd came up that way, and he thought he would settle down with George for a time. The newcomer, Tam Kennedy, came in after his day's work, and the two smoked in silence for two hours. Then Tam remarked: "Aw saw a bull doon the road the nicht."

Next morning George Broon said: "It wasna a bull; it was a coo."

Tam at once set about packing his bag.

"Are ye gaein' awa?" asked George in surprise.

"Yus," said Tam savagely, "there's far ower much argy-bargying here."

* * *

Summer holidays at last! Many a day I have longed for them, but now that they are here I feel very very sad. For to-day some of these bairns of mine sat on these benches for the last time. When I blow my bugle again I shall miss familiar faces. I shall miss Violet with her bonny smile; I shall miss Tom Macintosh with his cheery face. Vi is going to the Secondary School, and Tom is going to the railway station. They are sweethearts just now, and I know that both are sad at leaving.

" Never mind, Tam," I heard her say, " Aw'll aye see ye at the station, ilka mornin' and nicht."

" We'll get merried when Aw'm station mester, Vi," said Tom hopefully, and she smiled and blushed.

Poor Tom! I'm sorry for you my lad. In three years you will be carrying her luggage, and she won't take any notice of you, for she is a lawyer's daughter.

Confound realism !

Once I felt as Tom feels. I loved a farmer's daughter, and I suffered untold agony when she told me that her father's lease expired in seventeen years.

" Then we're flittin' to Glesga," she said,

and I was wretched for a week. She was ten then ; now she is the mother of four.

Annie and her seventeen years reminds me of the professor who was lecturing on Astronomy to a village audience.

" In seven hundred million years, my friends," he said solemnly, " the sun will be a cold body like the moon. There will be no warmth on earth, no light, no life.... nothing."

A chair was pushed back noisily at the back of the hall, and a big farmer got up in great agitation.

" Excuse me, mister, but hoo lang did ye say it wud be till that happened ? "

" Seven hundred million years, my friend."

The farmer sank into his chair with a great sigh of relief.

" Thank Goad ! " he gasped, " Aw thocht ye said seven million."

They say that when a man dies after a long life he looks back and mourns the things that he's left undone. I suppose that some teachers look back over a year's work and regret their sins of omission. I do not.

I know that I have had many lazy days this session ; I know that there were exercises that I failed to correct, subjects that I failed to teach. I regret none of these things, for they do not count.

Rachel Smith is leaving the district, and to-day Mary Wilson shook her hand. " Weel, by bye, Rachel, ye'll have to gang to anither schule, and ye'll maybe have to work there," she said.

" Eh ? " I cried, " do you mean to say, Mary Wilson, that Rachel hadn't to work in this school ? "

" No very much," said Mary, " ma father says that we just play ourselves at this school."

Mary's father is right; I have converted a hard-working school into a playground. And I rejoice. These bairns have had a year of happiness and liberty. They have done what they liked; they have sung their songs while they were working at graphs, they have eaten their sweets while they read their books. They have hung on to my arms as we rambled along in search of artistic corners. It was only yesterday that Jim Jackson marched up the road to meet me at dinner-time with his gun team and gun, a log of wood mounted on a pair of perambulator wheels. As I approached I heard his command : " Men, lay the gun ! " and when I was twenty yards off he shouted " Fire ! "

" Please, sir," he cried, " you're killed now, but we'll take you prisoner instead." And the team lined up in two columns and escorted me back to the school to the strains of *Alexander's Ragtime Band* played on the mouth-organ.

" Is it usual, Colonel," I asked, " for the commander of the gun team to act as the band ? "

Jim scratched his head.

" The band was all killed at Mons," he said, " and the privates aren't musical." Then he struck up *Sister Susie's Sewing Shirts for Soldiers*.

I know that I have brought out all the innate goodness of these bairns. When Jim Jackson came to the school he had a bad look ; if a girl happened to push him he turned on her with a murderous scowl. Now that I think of it I realise that Jim is always a bright cheery boy now. When I knew him first I could see that he looked upon me as a natural enemy, and if I had thrashed him I might have made him fear me, but the bad look would never have left his face.

If I told anyone that I had made these bairns better I should be met with the contemptuous glance that usually greets the man who blows his own horn. Stupid people can never understand the man who indulges in introspection ; they cannot realise that a man can be honest with himself. If I make a pretty sketch I never hesitate to praise it. On the other hand I am readier than anyone else to declare one of my inferior sketches bad. Humility is nine-tenths hypocrisy.

I do have a certain amount of honesty, and I close my log with a solemn declaration of my belief that I have done my work well.

As for the work that the Scotch Education Department expected me to do....well, I think the last entry in my official Log Book' is a fair sample of that.

" The school was closed to-day for the summer holidays. I have received Form 9b from the Clerk."